Valdar's Hammer

Terran Strike Marines Book 3

By

Richard Fox

&

Scott Moon

Chapter 1

A white abyss swirled before Admiral Valdar's vision. The chaos of a wormhole jump wreaked havoc on his eyes and equilibrium as the quantum bridge faded away. He put a hand to his helmet and waited long seconds as the universe righted itself.

The bridge of the *Breitenfeld* grew more and more active as crew recovered from the jump and sprang into their duties.

"We're in the Syracuse system," said Egan, the ship's executive officer, from a workstation to Valdar's right. "Sensors pulling additional data now."

Valdar slapped the emergency release on his chair's harness and lurched to his feet, still unsteady from the jump. He made it to the holo tank to the rear of the bridge and pressed his palm to a screen. As a holo field with the *Breitenfeld* at the center came to life, blue icons of friendly ships appeared behind and well above his ship.. at a distance further than anticipated.

"Enemy contact," called out Lieutenant Utrecht, the ship's gunnery officer. Red diamonds appeared in the holo tank, on a curved vector toward the ship. Valdar plucked one of the diamonds out and sensor data resolved into a Kesaht fighter, one shaped into a crescent. New contacts appeared, moving much slower.

"XO, launch the alert fighters. Guns, why haven't you worked together a firing solution for the rail cannons yet?" the admiral asked.

"Gun crews are—" Utrecht shook his head quickly, "—operating well below standards. They're engineers cross-trained to man the cannons, Admiral. They're not gun bunnies. That's no excuse but we're working on it."

Valdar's lips pressed into a thin line. The ship was operating on a skeleton crew. Most of the cargo space had been given over to the Keystone jump gate in the flight deck, his normal sailors replaced by tech experts who knew how to put the Keystone together and take it apart in mere hours, not how to fight in a warship.

"The Kesaht are not going to wait, Guns," Valdar said.

"Several chief petty officers are on hand making corrections." Utrecht put a hand to the side of his helmet. "I can connect you to the audio feed."

Valdar snorted, imagining the tirade of expletives the chiefs were unleashing on the hapless gun crews.

The slower enemy contacts resolved into Kesaht cruisers and their clawships, destroyer-sized vessels with energy cannons that could rip a hole through his hull with a single hit. The leading edge of the fighters were still several minutes away from firing

4

range.

"Sir, there's something…weird out there," Egan said. He joined Valdar at the holo table and an incomplete sphere formed in the holo tank, adjacent to the enemy's oncoming curved flightpath. Although nearly twice the size of Earth's moon, it was fragmented, like an exploded view of a natural satellite—a moon blasted apart from the center, but frozen in time as a larger sphere made up of jagged, enormous fragments.

"I'll agree with 'weird,'" Valdar said. "Can ships navigate through that?"

"Getting some odd graviton emissions from inside," Egan said, "but there's no reason a ship couldn't make it through…if their helmsman had nerves of steel and the captain something of a death wish."

"Assume the Kesaht have both," Valdar said. "Redirect the alert fighters to screen the moon. I hate surprises in the middle of a fight."

"What about the enemy contacts coming right for us?" Egan asked.

"We came here with allies," Valdar said as he ran two fingers down a screen and opened a channel to a ship in the Dotari fleet that had made the jump to Syracuse with the *Breitenfeld.*

A single alien appeared in the holo, his quills long and tipped with gray, his beak longer and with a pronounced tip. The Dotari looked at him with human-like eyes and raised an eyebrow.

"Valdar," the alien said, "you've decided to fight the battle by yourself?"

"No, Admiral Bat'ov, there must have been a small miscalculation in the offset jump from the Gamma Draconis gate. Not out of the ordinary when moving so many ships through a single wormhole," Valdar said.

"You've launched six of your Eagle fighters—*not* on an intercept course—and have *not* engaged your rail cannons," Bat'ov said. "You believe the Kesaht are *not* a threat?" The Dotari leaned toward Valdar and gave him a sidelong look.

"My ship is not operating with its usual crew complement." Valdar looked over his shoulder to Utrecht, and the massive rail cannons running down the top hull fired. Electricity snapped like lightning from the twin vanes on each turret as hypervelocity shells launched toward the oncoming Kesaht.

"Ah, good," Bat'ov said. "When you approached the Council of Firsts for aid in defending human colonies, we assumed you actually needed the help. Your ship is well-known for facing impossible odds, but to engage so many Kesaht with such a…hesitant response…made me curious."

"My guns are in the fight, Bat'ov. If you'd be so kind as to—"

"We have five squadrons of fighters in the void en route to the *Breitenfeld*." Bat'ov waved a claw-tipped hand in the air. "My artillery ships are already maneuvering to engage. See that telemetry data is shared so as to avoid fratricide. Any stray shots that might damage your noble vessel would bring great shame to us—a caste demotion at the very least."

"And I don't want to get shot either," Valdar said.

"Maneuver data will come to you via tight-beam IR."

"Then let us join the battle. Cod mittens," Bat'ov said and vanished from the holo tank.

"I'm done trying to teach them the right way to say it," Egan said, shaking his head.

"New contacts!" Utrecht called out, an edge of panic in his voice.

"His old man had a better grasp of that bridge station," Egan said to Valdar.

"We'll work on his command presence later." Valdar moved the holo to the oncoming wave of Kesaht fighters, and larger vessels shaped like cargo haulers with burning engines appeared.

"Troop haulers," Egan said. "I used to be a Strike Marine, sir."

"You want to grab a gauss carbine and get your hands dirty?" Valdar asked. "The quartermaster has the duty to repel boarders."

"The quartermaster ran a 3D print foundry before she came aboard," Egan said.

"We've got Strike Marines aboard," Valdar said. "They're up to the task."

"They better be," Egan said. The ship shuddered as the rail cannons fired.

"*Gott Mit Uns,*" Valdar said.

****

Warning sirens blared through the *Breitenfeld* as Lieutenant Hoffman ran down the passageway, his boots clanging against the metal decks. Nausea threatened to overcome him and his wobbly balance almost sent him bouncing off the bulkheads as he ran. There was nothing so unpleasant as a bad wormhole jump, but making a jump straight into a combat situation was a new challenge.

Vents opened along the ceiling and white strobe lights along the ceiling flashed. The ship was about to suck its air into storage tanks before the battle began. Hoffman pulled his helmet off the mag locks on the small of his back and put it on as he skidded around a corner. The opaque visor blocked his vision and he smacked into something. Hoffman stumbled forward as his visor switched on and he found himself nose to nose with an irate crewman.

"You jarheads know how to say 'make way'?" The crewman slapped Hoffman on the side of his helmet.

"Make! Way!" Opal thundered past the two, the doughboy's massive feet slamming against the deck. The rest of Hoffman's Strike Marines—Booker, Garrison, Max, King, and Duke—struggled to keep pace as Opal lengthened his stride.

Breitenfeld crewmen plastered themselves against the bulkheads as the last combat doughboy barreled down the passageway like a locomotive.

"Opal!" Hoffman got to his feet and took off at a run, darting around crewmen who were all moving with the same sense of purpose. Everyone on the carrier had a place to be during a red alert.

Opal glanced over his shoulder without slowing his headlong pace. He didn't see the cart loaded with cases that slid out in front of him, but he barely slowed as he crashed through them, scattering plas-steel boxes across the deck.

"Sir?" Opal asked without stopping.

"Watch where you're going and wait for the team!" Hoffman shouted.

Opal obediently adjusted his pace but concern filled his deep voice. "Red alert, sir! Red alert on the *Breitenfeld!*"

A squad of naval ratings jumped backward to avoid getting crushed. Hoffman and his team followed a few seconds later.

"We're going to catch hell from the Chief of the Boat, aren't we?" Garrison asked.

"Have we used the 'he's just a doughboy' excuse yet?" Booker asked. "This is the *Breitenfeld*, ship of miracles. I'm sure the crew's been through stranger things."

"Red alert!" Opal roared at people he passed. "Kill enemy!"

"Get some!" Garrison shouted. "I hope we get boarded. He'll be disappointed if it's just a drill."

Opal growled and ran faster.

"Opal!" Hoffman overtook King to get just behind Opal. "Match my pace. 'Make way,' remember?"

"Make! Way!" The doughboy's voice boomed off the bulkheads, the shout overpowering the warning sirens and causing the naval ratings to turn around en masse, like antelope on the savanna suddenly spooked by a predator. Without hesitation, they parted to make a path large enough for Opal.

Hoffman's earpiece chimed and an alert popped onto his visor screen.

"Yes, Admiral Valdar," he said, his helmet keeping the conversation private. He swallowed hard. Talking to the hero of the Ember War was still new for the lieutenant.

"You sound out of breath, Lieutenant. I appreciate the hustle. Set up security around the Keystone the moment you reach the flight deck. The device is mission-critical equipment. Don't let the enemy damage or seize it," Valdar said.

"Aye-aye," Hoffman said. "We expecting trouble?"

"Always. And the kind of trouble Strike Marines excel at dealing with."

"Shoot aliens. Break things. Roger that."

"*Gott mit uns*," Valdar said and closed the channel.

God is with us, Hoffman thought. Hearing the ship's motto sent a chill down his spine. He wasn't one to get starstruck…but this was the *Breitenfeld*, after all.

He switched to the ship's internal security channel. "Hammer Six to Armsman One, what's your status?"

Master-at-Arms Bartholomew "Bart" Fellows took a moment to answer. *"Standing by to stand by. I'll feel better with you and your team on the flight deck."*

"Be with you momentarily," Hoffman said, glancing over his team. Gunney King's face was set and determined. The team's head NCO had been tightlipped and focused since a pair of Ibarran spies had escaped from him on Koen. Despite King's self-proclaimed failure, he'd kept the Strike Marines ready and able despite the accumulated fatigue of back-to-back assignments and running battles against the Kesaht.

Opal continued to announce the alert to everyone he encountered. "Red alert! Opal run to battle station!"

"Man, I forget how massive Opie is," grunted Max, the team's commo specialist, as he adjusted his pack of extra gear locked to his back. The Strike Marine had been badly wounded by an Ibarran legionnaire and was still recovering from his injury, though he had yet to voice a single word of complaint.

Garrison, the breacher, followed close behind Max. "You know what we need? A really loud klaxon and flashing red lights. Maybe an announcement over the public-address system," Garrison said. "The air's about to get sucked out to stop fires and blast waves. We. Get. It."

"Shut your pie hole, Garrison," King panted. "Be more like Opal. He's a damn fine Strike Marine. Look at him clearing space squids out of the way. That's enthusiasm!"

"Red alert! Kill enemy," Opal said, pointing to the flashing lights he passed under. His shoulder clipped a sailor running the other direction, spinning the man into the bulkhead.

"Opal sorry to squid," the doughboy said without looking back.

Hoffman and his team emerged onto a walkway above the flight deck. The open space was cramped, the rear two-thirds being occupied by the massive basalt-colored blocks of the Keystone, the portable wormhole generator that could link into the Crucible gate network spanning most of the galaxy. The one-of-a-kind device had been instrumental in recovering a Dotari Golden Fleet in deep space and bringing back a cure for the phage killing off the race allied with the Terran Union.

The front third of the flight deck held Eagle void fighters and Mule transports, all swarming with crew and pilots as the ships readied for battle. The hangar doors were open, the force field between the void and the ship crackling along the edges.

A crewman inside a loader suit pushed a cargo container toward the Keystone and shut off the anti-grav plates beneath it. It came down with a heavy thump. A sailor wearing void armor and carrying a gauss carbine ran up and gestured angrily at the case.

"There's Chief Fellows," Hoffman said. "Gunney King, we're going to need more cover around the Keystone if we're going to defend it."

"And here I was happy to stop Kesaht bullets with my face," Garrison said. "Better to be a bullet sponge than let that thing get dinged, right?"

"I bet Opal could throw him through the force field from here," Duke said.

"Team," King said, slapping a magazine into his gauss rifle, "seal for void combat and sound off." He jabbed a thumb under the edge of his helmet and his power armor tightened against his body.

A chill went up Hoffman's spine as he listened to his

Strike Marines through their suit infrared laser comms.

"Booker, ready."

"Duke, born ready."

"Max, present, accounted for, and fighting next to Garrison under protest. He's always stealing my magazines."

"Garrison, ready and handsome in a rugged, not sissified way…and I need your mags. Maxy, as I'm a better shot than you."

"Opal, ready, sir."

"King. Sealed. Team checked out for void combat."

With his team combat ready, Hoffman pressed a switch under his helmet and a gust of stale air went over his face as his armor went to internal tanks. A small display of his life-support systems came up on his visor—green and at one hundred percent. Leaders were always the last to seal off before combat. If one of his Marines wasn't ready to fight in the void, it was his duty to get them ready, even if it meant sacrificing his own functioning suit to the Marine in need.

"Hoffman. Good to go."

The star field beyond the hangar shifted to one side, and a sliver of a distant planet came into view.

"Opal," King said, whacking the back of his hand against the doughboy's shoulder, "see those cargo pods? I need them moved to two meters in front of the Keystone."

"Yes, Gunney." Opal vaulted over the handrail and landed next to a pair of sailors.

The warning sirens changed their tone and air rushed into ceiling vents. Sailors and Hoffman's Marines double-checked the

seals on their void suits. Asphyxiation was a hell of a way to die—
and fairly embarrassing if the cause was a poorly checked void suit.

"*Breitenfeld*," came through Hoffman's ship-wide IR
channel, "*this is Valdar. We've arrived in the Syracuse system and made
contact with the Kesaht. Stand by for void combat.* Gott Mit Uns."

Max crossed himself and spoke a Templar prayer to Saint
Kallen. Hoffman saw this and frowned. He hadn't seen a single
shrine to the Saint anywhere on the ship since they'd come aboard
after the mission on Koen.

"Lieutenant," Chief Fellows called, waving up at the
Marines, "you want to be cannon fodder or you want to help out?"

"You think this squid knows what he's doing?" King asked
Hoffman on a private channel.

"His boat," Hoffman replied. "You think he needs the
wheel reinvented?"

"We'll go with the assumption he's not a potato of a
tactician." King grabbed the handrail and swung over. Hoffman
was about to follow when a tremor came through the deck.

"Rail cannons," Fellows said. "Baddies are closer than I
thought."

Eagles began launching in pairs as updates from the bridge
filtered through Hoffman's earpiece and across his visor. The ship
and his Marines were in for a hell of a fight.

Chapter 2

Kevin "Ax" DeVries banked his Eagle hard, flexing every muscle in his body and pushing his feet down as hard as he could to keep his blood pressure up. His flight suit couldn't squeeze any harder but dark spots still clouded his vision as he made a series of high-g turns. His wingman, call sign "Stingy," followed back and to his left.

DeVries took a hand away from his fighter's control panel and reached out toward a strange orb hanging in the void. The object blew up on his canopy display. It looked like an asteroid field…but one neatly organized into a sphere. Rocks the size of stadiums and capital ships hung motionless.

"There's something you don't see every day," Stingy said. "Does Valdar really want us to fly into that…thing?"

"The Kesaht aren't afraid to fly through it. Mission brief says the moon's held together by some Xaros tech. Might get some weird graviton chop, but no different than flying in the void. Come on, don't you want to tell your grandkids you flew through a shattered moon during a combat operation?" DeVries said.

"One minute we're doing joint ops with the Dotari above their home world. Next thing you know, we're roped into a deep-space battle to the death. I can't tell if the *Breit* is blessed or cursed," Stingy said.

Fragments of the moon—ninety or ninety-five percent of its original mass, according to the pre-flight briefing—floated in a cluster above Syracuse Prime, and DeVries and Stingy headed straight for the center of the loose sphere.

When the Pathfinder teams first surveyed the planet, they discovered that the original inhabitants on Syracuse had blown up their moon in their fight against the Xaros. It hadn't worked, as all trace of the defenders had been erased—standard operating procedure for the Xaros as they marched across most of the galaxy, defeating every race they encountered until humanity. The Xaros built Crucible gates over habitable worlds, but leaving the broken moon to rain down on Syracuse would have turned the planet into a hellscape. Exactly how the Xaros had stopped the moon's breakup was still being studied.

Following DeVries and Stingy were another six Eagles—all the fighters the carrier could muster for this fight. Behind them flew several squadrons of Dotari void supremacy fighters in tight formation. The *Breitenfeld* and her fleet of Dotari ships made for the planet at best speed.

DeVries and the fighters were to screen the capital ship's course through the moon. The fleet had already destroyed a number of small Kesaht picket ships, and Valdar wanted to use the moon to mask their approach. The worry was that the Kesaht had the same idea and had ships of their own coming to intercept the human/Dotari alliance.

"I can almost feel the gravity pulling that mess to the surface," Stingy said. "It's so weird—I mean, freaky, nasty weird. Wouldn't it suck to be down there staring up, waiting for the mother-of-all meteor showers?"

"Looking at it gives me a headache," DeVries said as he adjusted his flight path. "Same feeling the Crucibles give me. I hate Xaros tech. Now shut up and concentrate. Can't have the Dotty's outfly us…"

"Concentrating," Stingy said.

Expecting the massive moon rocks to drift apart, DeVries steered around the first piece and felt his stomach lurch as he jammed his control stick forward, then twisted hard right, then left to avoid debris he hadn't seen from outside the cluster.

Even though the seat of his Eagle had been custom fit to his body and his flight suit and his helmet was tight, he still felt like he was being tossed around in a roller coaster. His navigation panel flashed warnings and proximity alerts sounded inside his helmet as bits of debris peppered his canopy.

"Not your best idea," Stingy grunted.

DeVries didn't answer but cut his speed dramatically. Stingy, amazingly, was still in formation to his left. Both pilots swooped around a motionless rock the size of a Mule, then came back together.

"At least no one's shooting at us," Stingy hissed between clenched teeth. "Yet."

As they came around the side of an asteroid, DeVries caught his breath. Dozens of Kesaht ships came into view, the larger vessels looking like planks of loose bark hastily reassembled against the trunk of a smaller tree. Smaller landing craft with blunt noses and stubby wings charged forward on afterburners.

"The Admiral was right about the Kesaht," Stingy said. "I'm reading crescent fighters mixed into the landers…got a fight on our hands."

"*Breitenfeld*, this is Ax. You've got bogies and Kesaht cap ships inbound," DeVries sent back to the ship. "Prep for a knife fight soon as you cross into the sphere." He switched channels to the rest of the Eagles. "Squadron, priority target is those landers. Keep them off our ships and let our big guns worry about their big guns."

"Got to defend the *Breit*'s honor like she's our sister about to go on a prom date," Stingy said.

"Prime internal rails and keep the crap metaphors to yourself," DeVries said, swiping a finger against a targeting screen and locking onto a Kesaht lander. "Squadron, share targets and—"

Missiles streaked past his Eagle from behind.

"Damn Dotties," Stingy sent. "Next time tell us you're firing!"

"Reacquire targets!" DeVries grumbled as a Dotari missile blew up the lander he'd intended to destroy.

He opened a channel to the Dotari fighters and a cacophony of clicks and squawks filled his ears.

"First, this is Ax," he said. "Need you to share—"

"Do not step on me while I am giving orders," a Dotari said.

DeVries left the channel and locked onto a transport as Kesaht crescent fighters sprinted toward him. Flying beside individual Dotari was easy enough as the aliens adapted to Terran Union procedures quickly and easily. But friction ensued when they tried to work with a Dotari unit doing things their own way.

The capacitor level on his internal rail gun flashed and he fired, the recoil bucking his Eagle like it had just run into a wall. He pushed power back to his engines and accelerated forward to recover velocity.

"Never fire a rail gun on a full stomach," Stingy said. "Hit, by the way."

"My target's dead in space." DeVries zoomed his fighter's optics in on his target, which had broken in half and spilled humanoid shapes into the void.

Hits flashed in the Kesaht formation. DeVries sent vid screen captures back to the *Breitenfeld.*

"Definitely troop transports," he said. Toward the back of the Kesaht swarm were more troop ships, but each was guarded by a trio of crescent fighters in close formation. "What's in those?"

"Look like Rakka in the first wave." Stingy's voice dripped with hatred and disgust. "They're too stupid to feel pain. That's why the Kesaht pitch them into every fight like cheap cannon fodder."

DeVries' rail cannon readied for another shot.

"*Breitenfeld,*" he sent back, "we're not going to get all of them. We've got another rail salvo before their fighters reach us. We'd appreciate judicious aim from the fleet if you've got to fire through the dogfight."

"Big sky, little bullet," Stingy said. "That's what those punks in gunnery are thinking right now. They've never had a rail shot scream past them."

As if on cue, rail shots from the fleet slashed through the void overhead, a short line of burning dust following each like a comet tail.

"Eagle first," said a Dotari on DeVries' channel.

He fired his rail cannon again and switched his power to the fighter's gauss cannons.

"This is Ax," DeVries said.

"First Ax, have you ever fought in an asteroid belt like this?" the Dotari asked.

"That's a big fat negative."

"Then you had better big fat fly well as we have not trained for this either," the Dotari said.

"Roger, anyone that scrapes their paint against a rock has to buy the first round. Agreed?" DeVries jinked his fighter to one side and let off a burst of gauss shells that destroyed a crescent ship.

A bolt of energy snapped past his canopy and DeVries rolled to one side.

"A wager! Accepted!" the Dotari said and left the channel.

"I've got one on me!" Stingy shouted.

"Bank left and cut your velocity." DeVries flipped his ship

over and found his wingman being chased through the void. He gunned his engines and took after them.

In the distance, the Kesaht landers and their escorts accelerated toward the *Breitenfeld*.

****

Hoffman felt the *Breitenfeld* fighting through the soles of his boots. With the air sucked out of the hangar, there was no sound. The jerk of the main guns firing, the staccato rhythm of point defense gauss cannons, the sway of the ship maneuvering, all came through his physical connection to the deck.

The lieutenant looked over his Marines, all positioned behind cargo crates set up as hasty barricades between the Keystone and the closed hangar doors. Garrison shifted his weight from foot to foot, his gaze locked on the dead zone. Opal held his heavy gauss rifle at waist level. The doughboy was still, like a predator poised to strike at prey the moment it emerged from its hiding place.

"Rough way to pass a battle," King said from Hoffman's side. "Sitting around on our fourth point of contact while the squids do all the work."

"You think the navy ever feels like they're shirking when our boots are on the ground and we're the ones getting shot at?" Hoffman asked.

"Well…you never see them volunteering to get in the drop pods, pick up a gauss rifle and close with and destroy the enemy through fire and maneuver, do you? Meanwhile, when this ship gets shot at, *we* get shot at," the gunnery sergeant said.

"There's that," Hoffman said. "How's the team?"

"Duke's itching to get a replacement sniper rifle. He acts like he lost an arm back on Koen. Booker's doting on Max but he says he's good to go after his stint in the hospital."

"Is he?" Hoffman turned his head to the team's communications specialist at the end of the line of Strike Marines.

"Biometrics check out. SOP calls for time out of a combat zone after a hit like he took." King shrugged. "But SOP doesn't really account for a team hopping from warzone to warzone like we are. Hell of a war."

"If Max can't keep up or he's a liability in a fight…"

"Doubt it, sir. That Marine's hungry for blood and he wants to get home to his family. Opal seems a little off to me."

"Opal's fine," Hoffman snapped. "There's always some system degradation after damage. He's an older unit…takes a little longer to repair."

"Age," King muttered, "it happens to the best of us and to the rest of us."

The hangar doors rattled slightly and the Strike Marines and armed sailors throughout the hangar ducked against the barricades. Hoffman touched the screen on his gauntlet and swiped through feeds.

Electricity rippled across the hangar doors.

"I can't find an external camera," Hoffman said.

"Sir…" King racked a round into his rifle's chamber.

Hoffman, his eyes focused on his gauntlet screen, shook his head. "The ship's systems are not optimized for—"

"Sir!" King elbowed the lieutenant and Hoffman glanced up to see a black line of smoke and fire tracing across the hangar doors.

"Prepare to repel boarders," Hoffman sent to his Strike Marines.

Sailors manning strong points across the deck, near bulkheads and interior doors, scrambled for cover.

"Keep the Kesaht away from the Keystone," Hoffman said. "Don't let it get damaged. Admiral Valdar was quite clear on that point." He pressed a shoulder to the cargo pod and readied his gauss rifle. The slabs of the Keystone—the jump gate that would resemble a crown of thorns once fully assembled in the void— loomed behind him. The Xaros technology used in system gates would self-repair, but the human version of the alien equipment wasn't so resilient.

"I vote for us not being shot too," Garrison chimed in.

"It sucks," Max said. "In case anyone's thinking about stopping a round "

The black line on the hangar door had nearly traced a circle a few meters in diameter when it stopped suddenly.

"Maybe they changed their mind," Booker said. "The Kesaht equivalent of a ding-dong ditch."

A second point of fire and melting steel sparked to life on the upper half of the hangar doors, cutting through much faster.

"I'm going to shut up now," Booker said.

"They're not using burn cord to get through," Garrison said. "I think they're cutting with a thermal lance. If anyone gets—"

"Watch your sector and stop talking!" King spat.

"All I'm saying is I could use a new tool for my breacher kit." Garrison shrugged. "Professional pride."

"Opal," Hoffman said.

The doughboy bopped Garrison on the top of his helmet.

"If I had my sniper rifle, I could drill a round through the breach points," Duke said. "Instead, I've got this damn peashooter that won't even dent the hangar doors."

The second circle was nearly complete, and the first breach location flared back up.

"You think the sailors want you shooting a rail bullet that could shoot through five decks of delicate equipment?" Booker asked.

"Barely twenty meters from here to the door," Duke said. "Broadside of a barn. Even you could hit that."

"Old man's got jokes." Booker took a grenade off her armor and hooked a thumb into the pin. "Good thing I can take my anger out on Kesaht soon as they—"

The breach points exploded in a shower of sparks. Hoffman ducked behind cover as a slab from one of the hangar doors struck the deck and skipped into the cargo container to his left. The impact slapped the container against the Keystone, nearly crushing Hoffman and King.

"Gott mit uns!" sounded through Hoffman's IR network as

the sailors opened fire.

Hoffman stood and brought his rifle barrel over the top of his cover.

Rakka foot soldiers poured through the two breach points. The stoop-shouldered, powerfully built aliens wore void armor with helms fashioned into snarling faces. The eye lenses glowed yellow and Hoffman could almost hear the brutes' battle cry of "Rook rook!"

"Light 'em up!" King shouted as he opened fire.

Hoffman's rifle bucked against his shoulder and a gauss bullet smashed through a Rakka's helmet as it dashed across the hangar. Air and blood burst out of the cracked metal and the alien pitched forward as a grenade blast took out a group of attackers, spraying shrapnel and viscera against the hangar door.

A wild shot from the boarders hit the top of the cargo container and tore through the back of it, just below Hoffman's shoulder. The bullet whacked into the Keystone behind him.

He shifted his aim to the breach hole and fired several times at the aliens surging through. A force shield flared with each bullet strike and Rakka dropped to the deck unimpeded.

"Shift fire off the breach points," Hoffman sent to his team. "There's a—"

"Opal kill!" The doughboy flung his heavy gauss rifle aside and unsnapped a war hammer off his back. He put a meaty hand on top of the barricade and was about to vault over when Hoffman broke from his position and ran to Opal.

"Opal! Stand down, stand down!" Hoffman leaped

25

forward and caught Opal by the waist just as he got one foot on top of the cargo container.

Using all the strength his power armor could muster, Hoffman threw the doughboy to the deck. That he caught Opal off balance was the only reason he'd kept the battle construct from running into the kill zone.

The lieutenant pressed a hand against Opal's visor and pinned him to the deck. The doughboy's face was twitching, one iris wide and unfocused.

"Opal, combat reset. Order Hoffman one-seven."

Gauss fire snapped around them as the doughboy's head canted to one side, then the other.

"Sir," Opal said, blinking hard and looking at Hoffman, "unit is armed only with a close-combat augmentation."

"Your weapon's over there," Hoffman said, pointing. "Get it and—"

The deck shook and panic broke out on the IR network. Hoffman looked over the barricade. A Kesaht lander had crashed through the hangar doors, half caught in the breach. The forward section was a crumpled mess spattered with the remains of Rakka boarders that had been in the kill zone when it broke through.

Strike Marines and sailors picked off stunned foot soldiers.

"Hoffman, what the hell was that?" Admiral Valdar sent through the IR.

"Enemy did us a favor," Hoffman replied. Through the rent in the hangar door, he saw two other alien craft tumbling through the void, spilling Rakka into space. He looked over his shoulder to the Keystone. "Precious cargo sustained light damage."

The wrecked lancer in the kill zone lurched slightly, like it had been kicked.

"What the hell?" King slapped a fresh magazine into his rifle.

Something hammered the inside of the crude boarding craft like a dinosaur smashing its way free of an egg until a giant metal fist thrust a square-bladed sword through the fuselage. The weapon was a crude copy of the swords the armor were famous for carrying and was already chipped in places…and so thick it looked heavy enough that even a Strike Marine in power armor couldn't lift it.

"Ah…shit," Garrison said.

A suit of Kesaht armor unfolded from the wreckage of the lander, rising higher and broader than Hoffman or the others expected. Four meters tall, its bipedal form slammed hoof-shaped feet onto the deck. What looked like industrial-strength gears and hydraulic cylinders peeked from the torso and around each of the joints. Grooves were scraped through the crude paint from its struggle to break free. As red light pulsed from faux eyes, its Rakka skull-shaped helmet turned right and left, searching for enemies and venting smoke from forward curling horns. Electricity popped across its fanged mouth slot and black hydraulic fluid leaked like blood wherever a joint or pistol moved.

Hoffman wasn't sure where the inner pod—the enemy armor's brain—would be. Without that critical bit of information, killing or disabling the monster was going to be trial and error.

"Hit it!" Hoffman yelled, switching his gauss rifle to high power and shooting it center mass. The bullet sparked off the armor with no effect.

The monstrosity circled its arms like an athlete warming up for a fight, ignoring the gauss bullets pinging off its exterior. Slapping the blade of the blocky sword against the deck, it pried up a metal section and flung the deck plating at a Strike Marine position. It spun through the hangar like a shuriken, tearing through the barricade where Garrison and Max had taken cover, a corner bursting through the back of the barricade, missing Garrison's neck by inches.

Garrison fell onto his back and scrambled away.

"Where are the Dotari when you need them?" He kept crawling as the Kesaht armor stomped forward and kicked another cargo pod, which tipped over and came down on the Strike Marine.

"Opal, get your hammer!" Hoffman lined up a high-power shot on the Kesaht's head and hit it just above what looked like an ear. The alien's head tilted to one side from the impact, then slowly turned around toward the lieutenant.

Hoffman's rifle buzzed in his hands, the battery pack spent. He backpedaled and looked down to the grenades on his belt. All were fragmentation; none were anti-armor. He unsnapped a battery from his waist as the Kesaht broke into a run toward him.

"Watch the cross fire!" King called out as the monster raised its crude blade, nearly scraping the tip against the hangar roof, readying a swipe that would cleave right through Hoffman.

"No hurt!" Opal charged the Kesaht just as it swung its

sword. It tried to redirect the strike to the doughboy, but Opal jumped to one side and the blade buried into the deck. Opal tilted back and brought the war hammer down against the Kesaht's knee. The blow shattered gears and hydraulics, black oil spitting out like blood.

Opal ducked around the Kesaht as its leg gave out, the Kesaht slamming the palm of its other hand against the deck to stop its fall. Opal swung his hammer into the elbow, cracking it with a shower of sparks.

The alien armor's faux mouth opened and needle-sharp teeth as big as daggers bit toward the doughboy. Opal swung his hammer up and knocked the Kesaht's head clean off. The metal skull landed near Hoffman's feet, eye lenses blinking on and off.

The decapitated armor made a weak swipe through the air, still active.

Opal jumped onto its back and rammed the hammer into its torso like he was driving a spike home. The blow left a deep dent and the Kesaht flopped to the deck. Opal raised his hammer and pounded the metal again and again. The doughboy didn't stop until the hammer tore through the armor and a gout of liquid came out, turning to steam almost instantly in the vacuum of the hangar.

Opal thrust an arm into the hole and pulled out a Rakka brain run through with wires. He looked at it for a moment, then tossed it aside.

Hoffman realized his jaw was open and shut it with a click of his teeth.

"Hammer, need a status report." Admiral Valdar's voice came

through Hoffman's earpiece. *"Do you need reinforcements?"*

"Negative, *Breitenfeld* actual," the lieutenant said. "Hangar is secure."

King and Duke hefted a cargo container off the deck and Booker pulled Garrison out from underneath. The two Strike Marines let it fall with a thump that Hoffman felt through his boots.

Garrison raised a hand in the air, one side of his power armor badly dented.

"Ahg, not…pleasant. Where…what…this isn't Vegas…where am I?" Garrison mumbled.

"His armor still has atmo integrity." Booker knelt down next to Garrison and pulled out a med-sensor.

"Put me in, coach." Garrison tried to get up but Booker pushed him back down.

"Is it bad that I can't tell if he's normal or has massive head trauma?" Max asked as King started shouting orders to the sailors around the hangar.

Opal hopped off the dead Kesaht armor and locked his bloodstained hammer against his back. He picked up his heavy gauss cannon and reloaded the weapon with textbook proficiency.

"Opal," Hoffman said, going to the doughboy, "status report."

The doughboy's eye trembled for a split second. "Unit is functioning within combat pineapples."

"What?" Hoffman felt a chill go down his spine.

"Unit is functioning within combat parameters."

"*Hoffman, we have a breach on deck seven,*" Valdar said. "*If you're not shooting anything, get over there and deal with that situation.*"

"Roger, moving." Hoffman raised a hand. Garrison gave the lieutenant a thumbs-up.

"Hammers, follow me!" Hoffman turned and ran for a doorway, his Strike Marines on his heels.

Chapter 3

Valdar gripped the edge of the holo tank as a Kesaht blast hit a few yards off the number-two rail gun turret.

"Point defense, engage those fighters," Egan said forcefully into an open channel.

"Got an allied request to hold fire," one of the gunners replied.

Three Dotari fighters snapped past the bridge, so close to the superstructure and the bridge that Valdar flinched. Explosions flashed off to the ship's starboard side.

"Roger, guns," Egan said through a clenched jaw, "watch your targets."

Valdar swept a hand through the holo and the battle around the *Breitenfeld* came into focus. The Kesaht ships were damaged or destroyed, and the Dotari fleet had closed with the human strike carrier and combined into a single formation.

Valdar rotated the holo and brought the system's Crucible gate into view. The giant basalt thorns of the jump gate moved against each other like an ocean creature swaying in a tide. He opened a channel to the Dotari flagship.

Bat'ov appeared and a high-pitched chirp stung Valdar's ears.

"Victory is ours," Bat'ov said. "Our next objective must be—"

"The Crucible," Valdar finished. He traced a circle around the jump gate and tossed it to Bat'ov's hologram. "It's damaged. You see the cracks down the thorns in the lower quadrant?"

"It's off-line," the Dotari said. "Fortunate for us. Keeps the Kesaht from bringing in reinforcements."

"Hurts us just as much as it hurts them," Valdar said. "We need to seize it now and bring it online."

"My Marines have never assaulted such a target," Bat'ov said, "but we are aware of the theory behind such an operation. Easy, yes?"

"Nothing involving a Crucible is ever easy," Valdar said. "I have a team of Strike Marines aboard. They've trained extensively for Crucible seizures. Let my lieutenant lead the—"

"A lieutenant? A junior officer?" Bat'ov's quills bristled.

"He's battle-tested and just eliminated the boarders the Kesaht managed to—"

"*Captain* Caz'ul will lead the mission. Your leather head—or is it jar neck?—may advise."

Valdar bit his lip. Joint operations with the Dotari still encountered a good deal of friction, no matter how long they'd worked side by side with the Terran Union. There was a time and place to fight a battle like this, and with the threat of more Kesaht capital ships coming from Syracuse, the issue of who would lead the assault on the Crucible was not the hill he wanted to die on.

"Roger, Bat'ov," Valdar said. "I'll have Lieutenant Hoffman coordinate with Caz'ul."

"Agreed." The Dotari admiral craned his neck to one side. "Are you aware of the contacts coming from Syracuse?"

"Send it over," Valdar said, steeling himself for another battle in what was turning into a very long, unpredictable operation.

Chapter 4

Strike Marine Colonel Heinrich Fallon covered his ears as the energy shield dropped. Power converters hummed louder than ever; holding the defensive barrier in standby mode required more power than keeping it up and was twice as hard on the ears, despite the baffles in his helmet.

The recoil management system of the Orbital Defense Rail Emplacement T-45, known as Devastator to her crew, extended its barrel. A combination of grav plates and hydraulic dampeners lined up to accept the force generated when the rail gun fired. Eight graphenium-reinforced braces—thicker than a ground car and taller than a house—made it look like a giant spider that couldn't move. The bunker complex that sheltered it as he cycled the next round into place and cooled the barrel reminded Fallon of a spider's body or the carapace of an alien bug.

"All personnel, stand by! Shot away! Shot away!"

Looking toward a cloud of Kesaht landing craft and crescent fighters in the distance, Fallon caught a glimpse of the barrel bucking backward as a ring of energy haloed the barrel. The air between the gun and its target distorted from the speed of the quarter-ton round.

"Antony, report," Fallon ordered.

His forward observer, Strike Marine Lieutenant Rob Antony, responded a second later. "Direct hit, sir. Scratch one Kesaht heavy lander."

Fallon jumped onto the concrete barrier and raised vision magnifiers. A large ship, bigger than anything Terran forces would use to land assault troops, plummeted toward the planet trailing flames, ship parts, and what he liked to think were enemy corpses.

"Incoming!" warned Lieutenant Baer, his other Strike Marine team leader.

Fallon lowered the field glasses and stowed them in a utility pouch on his armor. The concussion of the incoming artillery shells staggered him. The ground jumped one, two, three times, rippling as shock waves passed through buildings and streets, shattering windows. Dirt and concrete exploded into the air from a dozen locations.

"Putting the shield up while the gun resets," said Master Sergeant Connelly, the weapon's crew chief.

Fallon put one finger on his forearm controls, keying his comms. "Put it up but decrease the diameter. We lose this rail gun, we lose the planet!"

Static from the next barrage of artillery shells hitting the nearly translucent energy barrier garbled Connelly's response

The retreating energy barrier left Fallon and his Marines

exposed as it slid back a hundred meters. Shells slammed into buildings and streets.

Lieutenant Baer waved his hands and shouted, frustration plain on his face. "Colonel! Get down!"

Shrapnel whizzed through the air, creating an atonal dissonance with the whistling noise of falling shells.

Fallon pulled a cigar from the cargo box of his armor, nursed it to life with a flame tab, and strode toward a hastily erected barrier. The defensive line was full of Strike Marines, militia, and civilians outfitted with mismatched weapons and armor.

He stood facing the enemy—a stupid, tactically irresponsible thing to do—and puffed his cigar. "We're gonna hold Syracuse Prime. These bastards don't know how bad they stepped in it. This is our system—our planet—and the full might of the Terran military machine is coming to kick these Kesaht losers in the balls."

Bounding behind the concrete barrier—which wasn't as high or as thick as he would've liked—he looked at his people without seeming to look, unsure he'd generated the effect he sought. They were either terrified or in awe of him. Maybe they believed his speech. Maybe they thought the desperate messages sent to the Terran fleet had reached someone.

What they didn't know was that he had pushed the boundaries of his authority and operational security protocols to send strategic, tactical, logistical details of the situation. If the Terran fleet came—*when* they came—they'd have no excuse but to come prepared.

"The clock's ticking, Baer. Remember my question about whether they'd be smart enough to set up artillery and suppress our rail cannon?" Fallon asked.

"They can't take it out. Not without bigger guns," Baer said. "Big pain in the ass though."

"Pain in the ass, my ass. They're going to drop more and more of those transports on us. I need that artillery battery silenced. There's about to be a clearance sale on human lives if we lose this position."

Fallon stepped away from Baer, whose size and Papa Bear confidence had an odd, calming effect most of the time but was slipping now. He needed to say something inspirational. Raising his voice, he emphasized his words with his cigar. "I've fought as part of the Atlantic Union Marines, during the Ember War and now with the Terran Union's Strike Marine Corps, a long time. Done my duty twenty times over. Stick with me and I'll show you how warriors get it done."

"Oorah," shouted Baer's team and other defenders.

"Brute determination and the unwillingness to die. We're a cancer to the Kesaht."

"Oorah."

"The Xaros couldn't kill us. Who the hell do these jackwagons think they are?" He marched down the length of the barrier. Most of what he saw was as good as he could hope for— men and women making do with what they had. The problem— the big, teeth-clenching, fists-ready-to-punch-something problem—was that only a small percentage of this group were Marines.

It was hard to tell the difference between militia and desperate civilians who'd volunteered (or been volun-told) to fight. He needed them to fight, much as he hated the idea. Best not to get to attached to them as individuals.

Baer walked beside him, his bulk making Fallon feel like a sawed-off runt. "That was nice, sir, photo-op worthy."

"Piss off, Baer."

The lieutenant laughed. "You need to give that talk to Lenton's misfits."

"Agreed. Let's go see them."

The Kesaht artillery drummed on the shield, the dissonant thudding causing men and women to flinch like nervous cats. All along the Terran defenses, defenders held weapons too tightly as they stared into the smoke and dying light.

Baer led him farther inward where a large group of Syracuse City militia and other civilians had gathered.

Gerald Lenton, city councilman, zone 12, stepped forward. "Colonel, some of us want to know the fallback plan," said the fit but disheveled leader, extending one hand to shake like they were meeting to discuss a bank loan.

Fallon left his hands on his hips, working his cigar between his teeth. "Pleased to finally meet you, Lenton. Thanks for helping defend the city."

"No problem, sir. It was a tough fight—"

"Was?" Fallon growled.

"I'm sorry?" Lenton said.

"It *is* a tough fight. We've only just begun."

"Well, of course. But there can't be many more of them. We killed thousands."

"Hundreds."

"Beg pardon?"

Fallon pinned the man with his hard eyes. "Thousands attacked. We killed hundreds, maybe less. That isn't what's important. What matters is we hold the line. If we kill all but one and that one tough bastard takes the rail cannon, they win. You think this is bad? Wait until their fleet can bombard the planet in earnest. Wait until a thousand transports hit the ground and dump out thousands of companies of their Rakka shock troops."

Color drained from Lenton's face.

"General—"

"Colonel. I'm not a general. I work for a living. Speak your piece, councilman," Fallon said.

"Yes, colonel. Of course. I was trying to say you're not very encouraging. My people are militia and civilian volunteers. They're not used to this. None of them signed up to die defending the city."

Fallon glared at him, thinking for some reason of his nephew, Lieutenant Rick Fallon. The kid had been cocky and arrogant, but fearless. He wouldn't be groveling like this show horse. Thinking of Rick made him think of Rick's father. God, he wished Rick Sr. were with him right now. This final campaign of his career—of his life—would mean something fighting beside his brother. And his brother would've known what to say to these people.

The Xaros took his brother, and his nephew, in the end. Not knowing exactly what happened to them haunted him. Rumors of his nephew's tortured fate fed the worst of his nightmares. He couldn't afford to think about it now—he had too much imagination and too few facts.

Lenton and the others stared at him, silent as lambs facing the slaughter.

"Whether you live or die might be up to you," Fallon said. "Whether you fight is up to me—and right now, everyone fights. Hell, bring your kids if they can fire a weapon. This is a battle to the last gauss round, the last drop of human blood, the last curse word. What do you think these space barbarians are going to do to the civilians—to your families—when we're gone?" He paused to stare at the hodgepodge fighting force one by one. "Without the rail cannon to defend us, the Kesaht will bomb us and land their entire invasion force in a matter of hours. We're fighting their vanguard right now, one artillery battery—"

A man in the front row of the militia dropped his head, muttering louder and louder in despair.

Fallon lunged forward, grabbed the man by the front of his load-bearing vest, and slapped him hard across the face—once, twice, three times. He paused as the man cringed backward, pulling to get away but unable to break Fallon's hard grip. One more slap across the face pissed the man off.

"That's what I need! Get mad! Get mad as hell and give it

to our enemies!"

The man chested up to Fallon, looming over him.

"You wanna fight me?" Fallon asked.

"No, sir! I want to fight the Kesaht!"

The defenders roared.

"What's your name?"

"Carlton."

"Okay, Carl, you just graduated my thirty-second boot camp. It's time to kick Kesaht ass—KKA."

"Yes, sir." Carl clenched his fists and bit his words. "KKA!"

Fallon faced the others. "Get to your assigned posts. Check your buddies, check your gear. We're going to hurt the bastards this time!"

Men and women hoisted weapons toward the air and cheered.

"Oorah, sir," Baer said as they strode to the next group of defenders.

"Yeah, oo-freaking-rah. We don't have time for hand-holding—you know that, don't you, Baer?"

"Yes, sir. But we're going to do it anyway."

"Was that too much?"

"I wouldn't have slapped him. Yelling would have been enough."

"I disagree. He's lucky I didn't ball punch him."

"That's why we all love you, sir. Not that many straight psychopaths left above the rank of lieutenant," Baer said.

42

"I'm going to ball punch you, you arrogant, back-talking, naval infantryman."

"It'd be an honor, sir."

"God, I love fighting. Gets my blood up!"

"You're no REMF, sir."

"Let's split up. Report any serious problems to me, then back to work. The Kesaht bastards are coming and we need to give it to them hard. And don't let me forget—you're about due a field promotion since your bosses, except Quinn, have inconsiderately gotten killed."

"Quinn isn't my boss."

"Yanking your chain, Baer. Just yanking your chain."

"Yes, sir."

It took Fallon several hours to inspect the defenses and he found the protective barriers smaller and shabbier than he'd hoped. Word of his pep talk got around, though, and soldiers and civilians shouted their desire to "get some" and "KKA" whenever he approached.

"We're with you, Colonel!"

"We're with you to the end!"

When no one could hear, he muttered to himself, "You're with me whether you want to be or not. No way off this rock. No help in sight. Nothing left but a chance to die on your feet."

His brother hadn't died well. How much better would he do? How had his nephew faced the end? How long could he really defend this rail gun that was doing a job that required ten guns?

Chapter 5

Hoffman peeked around a bulkhead. The *Breitenfeld*'s hangar was a mess of dead Rakka and the remains of the Kesaht armor. He stepped around the corner, rifle up, the stock jammed against his shoulder. His nerves were still raw and every dead alien on the deck struck him as a threat playing possum, no matter how damaged the body.

"Where's the fire?" Max asked from the rear of the stack against the bulkhead.

"Valdar said to get back to the hangar. Await further instruction." Hoffman relaxed a bit. The feed from the ship's command and control channel had slacked off after the local battle had shifted to the Terran Union and the Dotari's favor.

Crew worked at a massive gear on the port side of the hangar. A chief saw Hoffman and waved him over.

"Go," the lieutenant said. "I think they need some muscle."

Garrison mimed spitting on his palms and reached the gear first. Drawing a length of metal off his belt, he slapped it against his thigh. It snapped into a crowbar and he jammed one end into the rear of the gear housing.

"Opal, pull to the left on my mark," the breacher said. "Rest of you can try and bring your pipe cleaners to help."

"You in charge of the Hammers?" the chief asked Hoffman.

"Roger," said the lieutenant as he turned to face the exhausted-looking petty officer.

"Got a search-and-rescue Mule coming in." The port half of the hangar doors lurched open a few feet as the Marines wrenched the gear. "It's picking up you jarheads—sorry—Marines."

"For what?" Hoffman glanced at his gauntlet screen.

"Hell if I know. Word comes down to get the hangar open. I get the hangar open," the chief said.

"Hammer six, this is Dustoff two-two," came through Hoffman's IR.

"Go." Hoffman held up a hand to stop the chief from saying more.

"Be advised, still a risk of hostile fighters and fire," the Mule pilot said. *"Don't open the hangar and leave the* Breit *vulnerable. We'll open our cargo ramp. Y'all EVA inside. Roger?"*

"Team, cease work." Hoffman waved at King and the Marines stepped away from the gear. The centerline of the hangar door was open almost three feet, enough for them to get through.

"Got it, Dustoff," the lieutenant said. "We'll make the float. You have our mission?"

"We'll get further instructions en route," the pilot said. *"I'm in position. Get your ass in here before the* Breitenfeld *maneuvers and you're floating through the void feeling real silly."*

Hoffman went to the opening and saw a Mule a dozen meters ahead of the ship, the cargo ramp open.

"Marines, with me." Hoffman jumped into space and felt artificial gravity slip away. Swinging his feet forward, he floated into the Mule as the magnetic lining in his boots activated and he came down on the deck with a snap.

Max, Opal, Duke and Booker flew in without incident, but Garrison angled up toward the ceiling, waving his hands at his sides like he was trying to flap wings. Hoffman caught him by the ankle and pulled him down.

"Linings malfunctioned." Garrison kicked a bulkhead and a faint blue glow came off his boot. "Damn lowest bidder."

Gunney King hit the ramp, slapped a red button next to the hydraulics and stamped a foot against the deck.

"Loaded up. Moving," the pilot sent.

The Mule lurched forward as afterburners roared to life.

King went to an arms locker near the front of the cargo bay and pulled out gauss magazines. "What's the plan, sir?" he asked.

"Sounds like there's another fire we've got to put out." Hoffman was on his way to the ladder leading up to the cockpit when his visor blinked with a priority message.

On his screen appeared a group of Dotari Marines in power armor that resembled his own in many ways, but it was thicker and covered in adornments—gold edges on breastplates, diamond-etched name plates, and rings of Dotari symbols around their upper arms. Their helmets, designed to protect their quills while still allowing heat transfer, appeared exotic to Hoffman. He knew the color coding on the quill housings were unit designators, but he didn't know much more than that.

The Dotari in the front bore a circle within a circle rank insignia on his chest—a captain. Covering his right fist with his left hand, he then slapped his left palm on his right elbow—almost like a defensive tactics strike—and held it.

Hoffman mimed the gesture.

"Booker, I think the L-T's hurt," Duke said.

"Peacocks," Booker muttered, "look how pretty they are."

"Stow it, Doc," King said under his breath when the attention of the Dotari officers was elsewhere.

"Gold trim." Duke said—a statement, question, and condemnation rolled into one.

The Dotari captain turned away and spoke to the other aliens behind him.

"Their armor is just as functional as ours," Hoffman said after he muted his channel to the Dotari. "They've fought side by side with us since the *Breitenfeld* evacced them all off Takeni."

"That movie's a pack of lies," Garrison said. "You see how clean and happy everyone was? And real banshees are a hell of a lot bigger and scarier and a lot more interested in ripping people limb from limb in person."

"Maybe you should ask the Standish liquors guy to do

47

another cut of the movie," Duke said. "He owns the rights. Spent a fortune to put himself in the movie."

"I heard he was really there but they cut him out for some reason," Max said.

"You all want to keep flapping your gums or you want to get your gear set for the next fight?" King asked. "Fresh battery packs. Top off your air tanks. Eat. Since when did combat become a gossip session?"

"Oorah, Gunney," the Marines intoned.

Hoffman shook his head, slightly put off that the Dotari captain was spending so much time exchanging pleasantries with his officers instead of giving a briefing on the mission.

Activating his helmet speaker, Hoffman cleared his throat. "Sir, this is Hammer six. I have a team of Strike Marines aboard Mule—"

"Very good, Thomas Hoffman," the captain said, turning back to him. "I am Captain Caz'ul, First Tier, and I have operational command of the assault on the Crucible gate."

"The Crucible?" Hoffman's brows perked up. A Crucible assault was a textbook Strike Marine mission—but one that took days to plan and rehearse. "Do you—what is the concept of the operation? Is my team the breach element? Command node seizure? External security or—"

"Your team will act where assigned, Sub-Officer," Caz'ul said.

"What did that Dotty just call him?" Duke asked, his hands balled into fists.

Hoffman shushed him with a wave of his hand.

"Captain, my team has limited equipment," Hoffman said. "We may not have the gear for what you have in mind."

"That's why he's the lieutenant," Duke muttered. "He's the only one of us that'll remain diplomatic."

Caz'ul narrowed his gaze at Hoffman, then made a muted clicking sound. "Very well. Let us avoid bovine leavings."

The Dotari tapped his gauntlet screen twice and made a tossing motion toward Hoffman. A light map of the Crucible appeared between them.

"Yes, thank you, Sub-officer Hoffman." Caz'ul turned to one of the other Dotari as clicks and squawks of their language came over the line. "*Lieutenant* Hoffman. My mistake. My Marines will seize the command node."

An overlay with Dotari writing appeared on the Crucible. Hoffman recognized a few number characters, but the rest was gibberish to him.

"You will take your Marines-who-strike and prevent the Kesaht low-listers from going to-the-downtown." Caz'ul clicked his beak.

"Can you repeat that and clarify your intent?" Hoffman asked.

"Do you not see where your team is on the plan?" The captain touched a spinning blue square on the overlay. "The bolted-on hangar structure? This passageway is where you will prevent them from reinforcing the node during our assault."

"With all due respect, Captain, do we have intelligence on

the Kesaht locations in the Crucible?" Hoffman asked. "The service hangars are of human manufacture and meant to augment operations on the Crucibles. The location is vulnerable. The enemy is more likely to put troops in the thorns connecting to the node where the self-repair—"

"This is not for discussion," Caz'ul said. "My previous human liaison was a Ranger. He told me repeatedly that Marines-who-Strike are dense and require something called 'crayons' to understand complex operations."

"Sir, you want to get that Ranger's name?" Duke asked.

"I will use smaller words," Caz'ul said. "Speak slower."

"I understand your concept, Captain," Hoffman said. "But if we don't have a complete intelligence picture of the defenders, this mission will be more dangerous than necessary. Crucible thorns can move. They can connect different parts of the station to each other at a moment's notice. You think your rear has been cleared then you're up to your neck in hostiles when the station reforms."

"I have sufficient forces," Caz'ul said. "Do you understand your instructions?" The rest of the Dotari looked at Hoffman, their heads cocked slightly to one side.

Hoffman drew the moment out, debating the pros and cons of trying to fight through the differing standards in human and Dotari operations.

"You want me to fight my way onto the Crucible, secure this passageway connecting the hangar bays to the command node, and hold it to prevent the enemy from reinforcing the dome while you initiate a three-pronged assault."

"Yes, exactly. Why did my Ranger friend suggest Strike Marine intelligence quotients were near room temperature?"

"The time stamps on the assaults…" Hoffman frowned as he gleaned more and more of the operation. "You want this to happen simultaneously? Wouldn't it be better to isolate the command node first? Ensure you're attacking with overwhelming force? We should stagger the secure and assault phases. Keep it simple."

"We are not simple," Caz'ul said, his chin held high.

"That isn't what I meant."

"My assistant will note your objection in the log," Caz'ul hissed under his breath, taking his time and drawing the sound out for several seconds. The other Dotari officers looked at the floor and rustled their titanium-graphene sheathed quills within their helmet. "Do you now desire to whine like hatchlings or is the mission clear enough?"

Hoffman didn't need to know much more about Dotari body language to realize he was on thin ice.

"No?" Caz'ul asked. "Then our discussion ends. Sub-Officer Gor'al has more instructions for you." The Dotari captain's projection vanished and a much younger alien with very little in the way of armor decoration appeared.

"Most welcome greetings," Gor'al said. "I am sending instructions translated into English and I hope they are adequate. My family wishes to thank you for recovering the cure to the phage from the Golden Fleet. Many children owe their lives to you," the junior officer said.

"At least someone appreciates us," Max said.

"No problem, Gor'al." Hoffman opened a file the Dotari sent over. The operations overlay switched to English, but it was full of terms he didn't understand. Frowning, he sent it to the rest of his team with a swipe of his hand.

"These make about as much sense as Chuck Norris running a day care center," King said.

"Eighth cohort will establish a *schwerpunkt* on connection thorn bravo three," Gor'al said. "Your *sperrlinie* on the access tunnel will—"

"Wait, Gor'al." Hoffman felt a headache coming on. "Are you speaking German?"

"I am well versed in Jomini, Clausewitz, Rommel and several other precontact human military strategists. It was my focus of study." The Dotari's eyes widened with pride. "Are you related to the famous human singer Hasselhoff?"

"Can I get off at the next wrecked ship?" Garrison asked.

"Gor'al," Hoffman said, "the Terran Union military doesn't use...twentieth-century German terms. I need you to clarify several things. In plain English."

"I feel that German captures more of the nuance," Gor'al said, his chin upturned slightly.

"English," Hoffman said forcefully. "Now, show me on the overlay where the fallback security locations are."

****

Hoffman slapped his gauntlet palm against the top of each Strike Marine's helmet as he walked down the line of them standing in the Mule's cargo bay.

"Booker, Garrison, Opal, Max, King, and Duke…the gang's all here."

"Heartbreakers and life takers," King said.

"I'm glad we're not assaulting the Crucible proper. They're haunted. Ruins my appetite," Garrison said, holding his stomach.

"Pro tip: try chewing your food and stopping at thirds," Booker said.

"It's called a dirty bulk and you have to eat big to get big," Garrison retorted.

Hoffman locked the door and signaled the pilot that they were all in. "Our next mission is straightforward. Just a little Crucible assault."

Garrison and the others groaned.

"Listen up, Hammers. We've drilled Crucible assaults dozens of times. It's an alien structure and Crucibles act—"

"Freaking weird!" they said in unison.

The pilot's voice came through their helmet IR. *"Coming around the debris field. Have visual on the Crucible. She's a nasty mess. Want a peek?"*

Hoffman tensed inside his armor. "Send it. We all need to see this."

The sight of a Crucible gate always put things into perspective for Hoffman. The ancient technology was the

Syracuse's link to the rest of the galaxy. The remnants of the now-extinct Xaros were humanity's pathway to colonies around distant stars…this after the Xaros had nearly wiped every last man, woman and child out of existence.

At this distance, he could almost convince himself the crown of thorns was from another version of reality. No human would design something like that. That the miles-long thorns moved to adjust quantum fields and establish wormhole gates only made the structure that much more off-putting, like it was a living thing. Lessons learned from the first Crucible assault during the Battle of Ceres were still taught to Strike Marines.

Hoffman looked at his team and wondered—as he did before every battle—if he would be able to bring them all home. Had he done enough to prepare them? Was he strong enough? Were they strong enough? Was the plan—the very skimpy plan—flawed?

"That thing has seen better days," King said.

Hoffman leaned closer to the holo, adjusting for the increasingly bumpy ride as the pilot performed evasive maneuvers. Kesaht crescent fighters, Terran Eagles and Dotari corvettes swarmed the void around the Crucible. Capital energy blasts from the Kesaht ships and the fleet led by the *Breitenfeld* crisscrossed in the void. Stray shots struck the Crucible's giant thorns.

"Nice," Booker said, her tone loading the word with all the weight of profanity. "I've got a bad feeling were going to lose the Keystone *and* the Crucible…and be very stuck out here."

"No time to worry about that. Max, help Garrison get his

breaching charges prepped," Hoffman said, still watching the view screen.

The Mule slammed right, then down.

"Handling explosives here! Do you mind?" Garrison yelled toward the cockpit, adding in a normal tone of voice, "They can't actually go off yet, but it's the principle that matters. Sometimes I think we'd be better off without pilots. You can't tell me this ship couldn't fly itself."

"Be careful what you wish for, Marine," King said.

Tips of the giant thorns had been broken off and cracks ran along the thorns like miniature canyons. Hoffman reminded himself of the barely adequate briefing and the many training simulations he'd been part of. He stared without blinking, hoping to see evidence of what he knew had to be occurring.

Crucible gates were supposed to be self-repairing. He suddenly felt ridiculous for the terror he'd experienced when the Keystone had been riddled with turret fire from the Mule and battered by the Kesaht raiders. Yet…the portable version hadn't seemed to heal, or if it was healing itself, it was doing so slowly. That unique property of the Xaros-built Crucibles made boarding operations perilous—when the breaching holes started closing while you were still inside them…

Hoffman fought down a smile as he watched the Crucible gate reknit one of the thorns, the next growing back faster than the first. Booker, Duke, and King all started laughing with nervous relief.

Garrison stared grimly. "I'm going to need more burn

cord..."

"Had me worried there for a minute. Of course, that will cause us problems. We'll have to move fast after we cut a hole to get inside," Hoffman said.

"I can live with that," Booker said, still laughing. "I've never liked the idea of being lost in space. Not here or anywhere else."

"All right. Pay attention." Hoffman pointed to a small holo projection in the middle of the Mule's cargo bay. "The control dome is nestled between these thorns…here. Captain Caz'ul needs us to secure this passageway connecting the target dome to this bolted-on hangar. This here," he said, indicating the dome, "is our rally point if everything goes downhill. Not part of the captain's plan, but a standard improvisation. Any good Marine would expect us to rally here in an emergency."

"Lieutenant Gor'al didn't set a rally point?" Max asked, skimming through the extraneous details sent to his tactical arm-sleeve screen.

"If you get through the two-page introduction, let me know. Dotari planning doesn't take failure into account," Hoffman said, unwilling to voice his frustration out loud to the team.

"Read the more recent file Gor'al sent over. It almost makes sense."

A few minutes later, Booker shook her head—and not because the Mule was jumping this way and that, making the text difficult to read. "Dotari Marines are brave but I don't think they should be allowed to write in English."

"We know the mission. Good tactics are universal," Hoffman said, regretting the words as soon as they came out of his mouth.

****

The intercom chimed twice. *"Listen up, Hammers, this is your pilot speaking. We're thirty seconds from the objective and on course for a perfect deployment. Please make sure your tactical displays are upright and in the secure position and don't forget to tip your crew chief. Remain seated until we come to a relative stop, or somewhere in the vicinity where we can dump you out into the cool comfort of space."*

"This guy cracks me up," Garrison said, counting the coils of burn cord he'd secured on the front of his woven titanium-graphene armor. Once they were on the Crucible, he'd stick them to the surface of the thorn in the shape of a small door using double-sided, void-rated adhesion strips.

Hoffman stood, holding onto a wall ring. "Seal your suits. Check your buddy. It's go time."

"You heard him," King said. "Get it done. By the numbers. Smooth is fast, and fast is smooth. No mistakes, or I'll have you running the length of the *Breitenfeld* until you die."

The Mule came to a relative rest above a Crucible thorn, the length of which looked like a dark highway over the distant planet of Syracuse. Hoffman checked the drop zone from the end of the open Mule ramp and jumped out. Seconds later, he activated the grav liners of his boots. His landing was so smooth and perfect he almost wished he had messed it up. It was like he'd spent his good luck with one perfect landing.

The rest of his team came down in pairs, sticking their landings like they were a demo team for a dog-and-pony show back in Phoenix.

Garrison moved quickly into place with Max right beside him to provide cover. They bumped into each other.

"I'm trying to work here," Garrison said, his voice sounding tinny and far away as void radiation affected it.

"You're a bull in a china shop. Whose idea was it to send you to demolition school?" Max asked, sweeping the area beyond Garrison with his gauss rifle.

"I miss Adams."

"I don't. There was something off about her," Max said.

"She never cramped my style. Hung a lot of trash on me, but was always my battle buddy."

Hoffman and the rest of the team set up a larger perimeter around the breach point, standing with the grav liners in their boots at full power.

Overhead, fighters swirled in a dogfight and the flash of exploding Kesaht ships as Valdar's fleet brought more firepower to bear. The enemy had left a token force to guard the Crucible, but the vast majority of their ships were in low orbit over Syracuse, supporting the ground assault on the colony.

"Less talk, more cutting a hole so we can get in," King said, his comm channel crackling with interference.

"Yes, sir. But chattering helps me concentrate. Adams was

better at it than Max, or any of you fine, upstanding individuals. And Duke. No offense. First burn cord in place, ready to go," Garrison said.

Hoffman kept his mouth shut. He understood Garrison better with each mission. The constant ribbing and jokes of his fellow enlisted Marines worked for the ox-strong breacher. Officers joining in the shenanigans was a fifty-fifty proposition at best. He knew when to hang back and let King handle it.

Garrison retreated and put one finger on the ignition button housed in the left sleeve of his armor, right next to his tactical screen. "All set. Once I set this off, we have seconds to get inside. The surface is acting funny. I think we may need to move faster than usual."

"What do you mean 'funny'?" Hoffman asked.

"It changed color when I attached the first strip of cord. Hard to describe. Like skin getting goosebumps."

Hoffman didn't see anything that was weirder than usual. "Max?"

"I was watching my zone, sir. Can't make a useful judgment about Garrison's hallucinations."

Hoffman braced himself to enter and looked at each member of his team, then at Garrison. "No time for scientific inquiry. Opal, then me, then the team. Garrison, breach it."

"Fire in the hole." Garrison jammed the button, raising his weapon even as the cord ignited and sank into the thorn. The cord hit the atmosphere beneath the hull and the force of rapidly expanding air from the extreme heat popped the section within the cord's ring out like a cork. The hole rippled partially open, the gap rapidly resealing as the team started to move.

"No, no, no!" Garrison clipped his weapon to his armor, then yanked a cutting torch from his gear as he dropped to his knees. A blue glow illuminated his face as he worked on the thorn's surface.

"What happened?" King demanded.

"Charge was too weak or the Crucible's self-repair is working overtime. Either way, bad for us. But I can fix this!"

King balled a fist, then slammed it on his leg in frustration. "Fix it faster!"

"I'm warning you, this is going to heal itself way quicker than you think. I'm making it big to give us a couple extra seconds. I'd like it to stay open long enough to let the last man through, since I'm said individual."

He ignited a welding arc and slammed it into the side of the hole. Heat radiated out from the contact and the breach shrank much slower. The edges trembled as they grew to fill the gap, like black sand on top of an earthquake or metal shavings gathering on the surface of a magnet.

A hunk of the breach wall under Garrison's weld tip sublimated into dust and evaporated. He stuck the welder against a new section.

"Let's go!" Garrison shouted. "It's already stitching itself back together. It's like it's trying to fight me. Told you these things are haunted!"

Hoffman tapped Opal on the shoulder and pointed to the

breach.

The doughboy hesitated.

"Opal! Get in there."

"Dark!"

"Opal 6-1-9, obey the order!"

Moaning like a wounded bear, Opal jumped through the hole. "Kill dark place! Kill dark place! Kill enemy!"

Hoffman followed so close behind the doughboy he was almost walking on the procedurally generated fighting machine's shoulders. The rest of the team came immediately behind him, spreading out once they were inside the strange alien room. Every surface was semi-reflective black…until the surfaces moved like sand washed by surf, retreating and reforming in places.

"Haul ass, Garrison."

The breacher squealed as he squirted inside, the hole he had made closing around him like a rapidly healing flesh wound. He landed on his side with a *whoomph*. The passageway had atmosphere; just why that air hadn't come screaming out of the breach and into the void was one of the many mysteries of the Crucibles.

"I forgot how much I hate Crucible assaults," King said. "Max and Booker, set security on that corner. Acoustics and radar pings showing movement from that direction."

Hoffman took his own position, holding back a curse after reviewing his tactical display and his helmet HUD. A swarm of something was about to charge around the corner.

Opal squatted at the corner of the hallway in his zone,

hugging himself with one arm and aiming his oversized gauss rifle with the other. "Pause protocol 33-XD202-HTWDX147Z. Pause, pause, pause," he mumbled, his voice deep and fearful. A second later, he growled his regular mantra. "Kill enemy. No hurt sir."

Hoffman looked over his shoulder at King to see if his top NCO had noticed the abnormality this time. The man was braced for the swarm of...whatever was coming around the corner. Maybe he hadn't seen the doughboy talking to himself.

Although only seconds had passed since they entered, to Hoffman, it felt like minutes. "Opal 6-1-9, are you effective?"

"Good, sir. Fight enemy."

"Switch positions with Booker. We're being assaulted from this direction."

Opal and Booker switched places. Seconds later, Rakka war cries filled the space, their roar sounding like an avalanche of barbarians in battle armor far beyond anything their primitive tech levels could have put together. Worse than the impending fight was the mission clock running in Hoffman's HUD. He couldn't afford another delay.

As though on cue, Caz'ul requested a situation report via text.

Gor'al had told Hoffman to simply send the number 1 as an answer if the mission was proceeding to plan. Gor'al had looked at him funny when the Marine had asked what number to send if things spiraled out of control.

"Rook rook!" echoed through the hallway and Hoffman pressed one shoulder against the gently curved walls of the

Crucible, just behind a kneeling Booker.

"Garrison, launch smoke at the intersection," King said. "Switch to thermals."

Hoffman touched the side of his helmet and a heat map of the hallway projected onto his visor. Garrison loaded a canister into the grenade launcher attached to the bottom of his gauss rifle and fired a smoke grenade. It smacked into a Rakka's face just as the alien rounded the corner.

"Whoopsie." Garrison unloaded much deadlier gauss bullets into the Rakka as a wave of gray smoke filled the intersection.

Hoffman and his team picked off the aliens as they struggled through the confusion of the smoke and over dead bodies.

An IR link full of static filled Hoffman's ears as Caz'ul spoke, the Dotari officer sounding out of breath and agitated. "What is your status, Marine of strikes?"

Hoffman emptied his magazine and slapped in another, hoping the snap of gauss fire would convey the situation.

"We're in contact with the enemy." Hoffman aimed and fired at the first Rakka to struggle through the smoke cloud.

The captain didn't respond.

Gauss rifles cut down the Rakka, but the sheer weight of bodies kept their charge going. Hoffman looked up at the breach point—fully repaired and solid. Behind them, the hallway extended another hundred yards.

"Fall back, keep up the fire." Hoffman slapped Booker on

the shoulder and she swung around and ran behind him, tossing a frag grenade to the Rakka as a parting gift.

Opal stepped into the middle of the hallway and braced himself against the floor. His heavy rifle, fed from a box of linked bullets, went full auto, the doughboy's immense strength keeping the recoil from pulling the muzzle higher. When his weapon clicked empty, the doughboy grunted, one hand reaching back to his hammer.

"Oh no you don't." Hoffman grabbed Opal by the carry handle on the back of the doughboy's shoulders and jerked him back. Opal turned and ran back to the next firing point the Marines had set up, reloading as he went.

The wave of Rakka receded, their war cries shifting to high-pitched yelps like wounded dogs. Hoffman fell in behind Booker along a wall.

"This…this doesn't fill me with confidence," she said.

The Crucible shifted beneath their feet, and Hoffman felt like he was in a moving elevator.

"The station's reforming." Hoffman looked at his gauntlet screen, but there was nothing from the Dotari assault elements. "But who's doing it? Caz'ul or the enemy?"

The pile of alien bodies at the intersection shifted and the junction closed off as the walls filled in.

"Now we're fighting in a maze," Duke said. "Just like Strike Marine selection."

"And how'd we all get through that test?" King asked. "Situational awareness and…"

"Violence of action," the team said as one.

"Three-sixty perimeter," Hoffman said and moved into the middle of the hallway. His team formed a circle around him, weapons pointing outward. He opened a wide-band IR channel. "Captain Caz'ul, this is Hammer Six. Our movement corridor is in flux, how copy?"

The thorn came to a stop with a gentle rocking and the sound of sand cascading down a dune filled the hallway.

"I hate this spooky shit," Garrison said. "Where's it coming from?" He looked straight up and gave off a startled cry, falling onto his back and firing into the ceiling.

Hoffman's gaze snapped high just in time to see a Rakka fall from a growing hole and onto him. He struck out with his rifle stock, crushing the Rakka's face and tossing the body aside and against Opal's back.

Claws raked across his visor and smacked his head to one side. Hoffman backpedaled and popped the Ka-Bar bayonet blade out of his gauntlet housing. He made a blind stab and the blade bounced off an alien's arms without cutting its armor. A side tackle sent him to the ground and a hairy hand slapped over his visor.

Grunts and curses from the sudden melee were Hoffman's only clue to the battle. Blows struck his chest and abdomen as he fought to bring his knife into the fight, but that arm was pinned to the ground. His rifle lost to the scuffle, he grabbed the Rakka's wrist with his free hand and used his armor's pseudo-muscle layer to augment his strength as he squeezed. Bones snapped and he jerked the hand off his face.

The bestial face of a Rakka leered at him, teeth bared and drool falling onto Hoffman's visor.

The lieutenant let go of the alien's wrist and grabbed it by the crude armor on its chest. He pushed the alien back, then jerked it toward him. Bringing his chin to his chest, he smashed the Rakka's face against the top of his helmet. There was a satisfying crack and a splatter of blood against his visor.

The Rakka lifted into the air and Hoffman thought the hallway's artificial gravity had cut out.

Opal held the bloody Rakka overhead then slammed it across his knee, cracking its spine.

"Hammers! Hammers!" a Dotari voice yelled through Hoffman's IR.

The lieutenant got up. The passageway in the ceiling through which the Rakka had attacked was resealing. Dead Rakka littered the floor, but all his Marines were on their feet. He picked up his rifle and saw a new passageway behind them.

"We should move," King said. "They know where we're at."

"Caz'ul, ping me your location." Hoffman shook blood off his bayonet and snapped it back into the forearm housing.

An icon appeared on his visor, just beyond the new passageway opening.

"Hammers are moving to you." Hoffman raised a hand next to his head and thrust it toward the other tunnel. His team moved out at a run, automatically falling into a wedge formation.

"Moving," Garrison said, rushing forward to fall in a few

paces behind and to the left of Max.

"Now I miss Adams," Max said. "Since when does the comms guy get stuck on point?"

Garrison disappeared from Hoffman's view as he and Max went around the corner. "You scared?"

"No. Just pointing out this is screwed up. Particularly while I'm on point. Already been shot once this week."

"Don't quit your day job," King said, his voice heavy with disapproval despite the slightly emotionless quality of all helmet commlinks. "Focus on the mission. This should be a short trip unless that Mule pilot put us down in the wrong place."

"We're at the passage to the control node now," Garrison said, pointing to an English-language sign over an arched door. "Guess the Rakka didn't care to redecorate."

Hoffman glanced at the sign as he passed it and frowned.

"That's not right," he said. "We're in an access corridor that doesn't even lead to the hangar."

"We're fighting a maze, sir," King said.

"Even with a reconfiguration…" Hoffman felt a chill spread through his stomach. "I think the Mule set us down in the wrong spot."

"Then which Rakka did we just exterminate?" Duke asked. "Don't they keep their security element in the hangar?"

"Bad assumptions lead to bad plans," King said. "What a cluster."

"Stop there." Hoffman pointed to a shut doorway, the seams of the obsidian-colored and textured doorway faintly visible.

He put a hand to the surface as the gunshots carried faintly down the hallway.

"Fight is on the other side of this door," the lieutenant said. "Garrison, blow it."

"Whoever's on the other side is about to have their day ruined." The breacher swung a bag around from the small of his back and pulled out a denethrite blast charge the size of his fist. He gripped his fingertips into the middle and pulled it into a net with a thick border, all made of the explosive material.

"It's Kesaht." Duke tapped the side of his helmet. "Their firearms make a distinct sound."

"Works for me." Garrison tucked the edges of the charge into the door frame. "Everyone sealed up? Overpressure from my skeleton key ain't going to be pleasant."

"Don't even joke about that," Booker said. "I can't fix burst eardrums and squished eyeballs."

Hoffman retreated from the rigged door and put his back to the wall. "Watch your targets when we get through. Don't want to hit Dotari. Ready when you are, Garrison," he said.

"Someone want to tell that to the Dotties?" Duke asked. "That's your cue, Max."

"I've got no contact with them," the commo Marine said. "Let's hope my non-Rakka good looks can get the 'don't shoot me' message across."

"Fire in the hole!" Garrison held up his detonator.

The denethrite exploded with a crack. The blast wave hit Hoffman like a slap and a chunk of the doorway ricocheted off the opposite wall and fell at his feet. It crumbled into the floor and vanished.

Hoffman fell in behind Max as he followed the stack through the blasted doorway, the edges already creeping back toward the center line. He stepped over Rakka bodies and felt relieved that Duke's heating was on point.

Gauss rifles snapped as the Marines finished off Rakka stunned by the breaching charge.

Gunfire sounded around a corner to a curved hallway but Hoffman recognized the outer perimeter of the jump gate's control node. They were close.

Garrison pushed the muzzle of his rifle around the corner and video from a camera mounted on one side sent images of Rakka and Sanheel—the taller, centaur-like officers of the Kesaht ground forces—near an open doorway leading to the control center. Rakka hacked at the edges of the door with crude axes to keep the doors open while the station tried to repair the damage.

A bullet from inside the command center hit an ax-wielder in the face and the Rakka crumbled to the deck. A Sanheel grunted a command and other Rakka dragged the body away while another of the brutish aliens took up the ax.

A Sanheel hefted a massive machine gun over the edge of the broken door and sprayed bullets then jerked the weapon back as return fire chipped away at the door.

"Frags." Hoffman took a grenade off his belt and pulled the pin. He and Max lobbed the explosives around the corner as King and Booker followed suit a few seconds later, staggering the attack.

There were hurried orders from a Sanheel before a pair of explosions broke down the hallway. Hoffman half raised his rifle and began to turn around the corner as the next wave of blasts came.

He charged toward the enemy, smoke curling around the ceiling and over injured Rakka and a Sanheel lying on its side, its four legs broken and bleeding.

Max drilled a pair of shots into another Sanheel's chest and it pitched back to the floor just before pounding hooves sounded down the curved hallway.

"Incoming!" Hoffman moved to a doorway for cover. Opal and Booker joined, Opal over top of him, Booker taking a knee to lean out and then around to shoot.

Three Sanheel charged around the corner, trampling Rakka without care. Two carried stubby machine guns, and the center alien had a spear cocked beneath an elbow.

Hoffman fired and his bullet flashed off a Sanheel's energy shield. The three aliens closed fast, their face shields carved into the visage of a snarling Kesaht demon.

Opal's heavy gauss opened up and overloaded the shield of a Sanheel. Shots tore through its torso and splattered blood against the walls.

"High-power shots!" King shouted and his rifle snapped with a plume of electric flashes from his muzzle. Another Sanheel went down with a sharp cry while the Sanheel with the spear closed, the shining tip of its weapon trained on Hoffman.

The lieutenant stepped away from the doorway and into the middle of the hallway as his weapon charged up.

"Sir, down!" Opal shoulder-checked Hoffman off his feet and into the opposite wall behind Garrison, then grabbed the handle of his war hammer and bent forward suddenly, hurling the weapon end over end.

The weighted metal end broke through the Sanheel's shield and buried itself in the alien's helmet. The Sanheel stopped like it had hit a wall, its spear dropping to the deck with a clang. It toppled over to one side, the hammer haft protruding like a horn.

The hallway was oddly silent.

Opal went to the dead alien, put a foot to the corpse and yanked his hammer out with a snap of broken armor. He tapped the haft against his shin, attempting to get rid of some of the gore.

"Who needs armor?" Max asked. "We have a doughboy."

Dotari language came from the broken doorway as it reknit itself.

Hoffman hurried past Opal and over the dead Rakka and Sanheel in the hallway, kicking a blood-covered Rakka when its hand twitched. The blow thumped against its side, but the alien didn't respond.

Hoffman put his back to the wall near the door and knocked three times quickly, then twice more with a second between each hit.

"You think they read their own commo annex?" Max asked.

"At some point, things might go well for us," Hoffman

said.

"Don't know about that, sir," Garrison said. "Remember all those banshees chasing us on that Dotari ship? We've been on a losing streak since we set foot on that place."

"If we have to beat this door down, we're doing it with your face," King grumbled.

The door cracked open slightly and Garrison raised a hand and gave a faint cheer.

"Terran Strike Marines!" Hoffman shouted and the door opened farther. A Dotari hand waved them inside.

The command center was a wide bowl with several tiers leading to a dais at the bottom. The ceiling looked like raw space, a projection on the dome better than any screen Hoffman had ever sceen.

Dotari Marines hunkered down around shot-up workstations, their wounded and dead lying behind defenders. Chirps and moans sounded gently through the command center as the doors shut behind Hoffman and his team.

"Sir?" Booker lifted her chin toward a group of Dotari giving aid to one of their wounded.

"Do what you can," Hoffman said. "Max, get comms to the *Breitenfeld.*"

"On it." Max pointed to a workstation and jogged to it.

Hoffman tapped a Dotari Marine, its chest armor scratched up and dented, on the shoulder.

"Where's Captain Caz'ul?" he asked. The Dotari pulled away and hissed at him.

"Marine." A Dotari bearing the rank of lieutenant banged the stock of his weapon against the ground. When he did it again, more Dotari joined, beginning a slow tempo.

Gor'al stood up from near the command dais and brandished his rifle overhead, his singsong words echoing off the walls.

"They don't seem happy," Garrison said.

"Sir," Booker said, backing away from the group of Dotari and shaking her head. "I found Caz'ul."

Hoffman went over to her. The Dotari captain lay dead on the floor, his armor cracked open and spattered with blood.

"Where were you?" a Dotari officer asked. "We were counting on you."

Hoffman saw the anxiety and fear on the young alien's face and felt a worse confrontation brewing as the bang of their weapons petered out and Gor'al kept speaking in Dotari.

"We need…we need to secure this station and contact the fleet," Hoffman said. Casualties were always hard to deal with, especially after the loss of a leader. Strike Marines were trained to fight through the shock and the grief. Just how the Dotari would fare right now…

"Did you cut off the hangar bay?" the Dotari officer asked.

"We were dropped in the wrong location," Hoffman said. "We managed to—"

The Dotari hissed at him like a cat.

"You mean no offense to our once captain," Gor'al said as he hurried up the wide steps leading up from the dais. "No offense,

Hoffman. Say *twee aga nas shik.*"

"What?" Hoffman frowned.

"Say it. Say it." Gor'al's eyes went wide.

Hoffman repeated the words as best he could, and the angry Dotari looked away from him and back to Caz'ul's body.

"Lieutenant Hoffman, sir, I have an encrypted message from *Breitenfeld* Actual," Max said, his gauntlet plugged into a shot-up workstation.

"Put me through." Hoffman stepped away from his team and the Dotari, glad for the opportunity to defuse the situation.

"*Breitenfeld* Actual for Hammer Six, are you receiving?" Admiral Valdar's holo appeared on the inside of Hoffman's visor.

"Hammer Six, reading you loud and clear."

"Do you have control of the Crucible?" Valdar asked.

"There's a lot of damage, sir. We have eliminated the Kesaht element and are treating injured." Hoffman watched the Dotari as he said this, knowing that his team couldn't keep getting this lucky. He was going to lose someone. The thought hung over his head like a black cloud though he tried to ignore it.

Remembering Opal's strange muttering and inconsistent behavior, Hoffman searched for the doughboy and found him standing on the raised dais, his huge gauss rifle held at port arms. He recognized guard mode. Normal. The doughboy was acting exactly as he should.

"We've achieved local void superiority and are transferring technicians to man the Crucible," Valdar said. "The engineers tell me the station will be off-line for days if it self-repairs. My ship's full of Crucible techs, thanks to the Keystone. I'm sending over enough to cut that timeline down."

"We'll escort the techs," Hoffman said.

"Negative, Hammer." Valdar shook his head. "Load up on the Mule I'm sending over. I need you and your Marines back on the *Breitenfeld*."

"Roger, Admiral. The Dotari element took a number of casualt—"

"Yes, I've already got an earful about that." Valdar's face fell. "We'll discuss that soon as you're aboard."

Dread pricked at Hoffman's heart.

"King," Hoffman said, raising his hand to get the sergeant's attention, "we're moving out. Back to the ship."

"Never a dull moment," Duke said.

A low, mournful song rose from the Dotari.

"You heard the lieutenant," King said. "Form up and keep your head on a swivel. Still might be Kesaht stragglers in this damn place."

Chapter 6

Fallon's stomach rumbled faintly with hunger. He was so exhausted that he wasn't sure when he ate last. He felt through his kit for a ration bar as he walked back to the rail cannon bunker from the outer trench line.

Empty.

His stomach constricted.

He pulled out a very short cigar and chewed on one end as he marched forward.

Three men and two women were stationed inside Devastator's fortifications, despite his desperate need for their rifles and combat skills on the perimeter. The building was two-thirds underground and thicker than the hull of a battleship. The barrel of the weapon pointed into the sky while the essentials—power converters, recoil management systems, and shell magazines—were kept safely underground until it was ready to do work. It would push upward, aim, and fire. Recoil would drive it back into hiding.

Stepping around the bolted-down feet of Devastator's

support columns, he saw no guards. Everyone inside was a Strike Marine, except for Jeffries and Cortel, who were retired Pathfinders. They posted their own watch when needed and monitored security cameras round-the-clock. If the enemy made it this far, they were all screwed in any case.

As the centerpiece of his defensive strategy and the most heavily defended position in the city, it was also where Fallon had put his best communications gear.

"Come in, Colonel," Captain Quinn said. "We're making progress."

"Good."

"Right this way." Quinn led him underground to a large room where they were fitting communication relays to a rocket.

"That's it? I thought it would be bigger," Fallon said.

"No need, sir. The smaller, the better, in fact. I'm hoping the Kesaht won't even shoot at this when we launch it and won't be able to hit it if they try."

"You're doing good work. Finish and get into the fight," Fallon said.

"Sir, this is our only real chance to survive. If this can't send a message through the Crucible gate, we're done," Quinn said.

"Maybe, maybe not. Paulson believes help is already on the way. He sent conventional messages after the first Kesaht arrived and before they attacked. He sent his own version of what you're doing. Nothing changes. We hold off the Kesaht with the rail gun until the fleet arrives and takes control of the system."

"Paulson's MIA." Quinn said. "I know what he did. That's

where I got the idea."

"Probably KIA. Let's not beat around the bush. Send up the rocket and have it launch whatever techno-wizardry you've put in it, and get back in the fight. Rail cannon, Captain, that's your mission in life until I tell you otherwise. Focus. Do the one thing that needs doing most. Win the day."

"Someone needs to be here in case there's a response—one of the retired Pathfinders. That's what I'm thinking."

"If the response isn't a fleet of warships and a crap-ton of Marines, it doesn't matter. Finish this job and get back to work. I need men out there fighting. End of discussion." Fallon returned the captain's salute and stepped toward the door. Pausing with his hand on the security keypad, he looked back. "Quinn, how will we know when they arrive?"

"I think I can detect ships—in a general sense—through the ionized atmosphere," Quinn said.

"You think?"

"Yes, sir." He fiddled with something on his work table to avoid Fallon's intense gaze. "It's like you said. None of it matters unless the response is a large QRF. Something on the order of armor."

Fallon grunted. "They'll send Marines and that'll be enough. I'll see you on the front line."

****

Colonel Fallon put in an eighteen-hour day before he took

a break, eating only twice during that time, and neither meal had been particularly satisfying. He would sleep for four hours, then do it again.

On easier assignments, he'd fallen into the habit of drinking a glass of scotch whiskey and reading a good book to fall asleep. It was his secret pleasure to read from actual paper pages. He liked the feel of them in his hand. Histories and biographies were his favorites—maybe a good bug-hunt story if told well—but he took whatever he could get. Falling asleep in his chair with a heavy book on his chest was the best part of his day—or had been before he took his current assignment.

Since arriving on Syracuse Prime, he'd forgone both hobbies. The planet was raw and untamed—a definite frontier world needing his constant attention. Now it was a fight for survival every minute of every day against an armed enemy, not the environment.

Less frequently, he read the report of his nephew's final mission. Most of the details were redacted by Admiral Valdar, hidden, despite Fallon's level-one security clearance.

He'd earned a reward by surviving another day, though few people would think reading *the report* an easy thing, much less a reward. He stared at the photograph of his nephew in his dress blues. Rick had been the son he never had, especially after his father died.

Although Fallon needed to sleep, he spent almost an hour reliving fights and arguments he'd had with his nephew over the years.

"Were you a good Marine, Rick?" Fallon asked the ceiling. "No, I don't think you were. If you were worth a shit, you'd be here helping me right now. No, that's unfair. But fair doesn't matter. Fair is for losers too weak to make their own rules."

Rick had complained that the other lieutenant in his Strike Marine company had it too easy. Thomas Hoffman was privileged, spoiled. The brass let him keep a doughboy that should have been put down a long time ago. They allowed him to steal his best NCO despite a freeze on transfers. Fallon had hated when his nephew complained like a common victim. He remembered yelling at the kid to just put Hoffman in his place, show him who was top dog.

He didn't sleep well, but he did achieve something like unconsciousness for three hours.

Chapter 7

Hoffman passed a pair of armsmen outside the ship's bridge, suddenly aware of the blood and gore he hadn't quite scrubbed from his armor during the walk from the flight deck. His breath smelled like nutrient paste and stubble grew where he hadn't shaved since yesterday morning. He'd never felt so un-squared away—which was exactly what he didn't need when facing Admiral Valdar and the captains of the Dotari fleet.

"Nice job on the flight deck, sir," one of the sailors said.

"Thanks," he said, distracted. He went to Admiral Valdar at the large holo table to the rear of the bridge and saluted.

Valdar, true to navy tradition, did not return the salute.

A group of Dotari ship commanders and Marines were in the holo table, a mute icon floating next to each of their heads.

Valdar, facing the crowd of projections, rubbed his beard. "Hoffman," he said, lowering his hand to point at the holograms, "be warned. They're in a mood today."

The *Breitenfeld*'s executive officer, Egan—once a Strike Marine before he succumbed to some insidious desire to become a naval officer—joined the two.

"Course is laid, Admiral," Egan said. "Waiting your order."

"First things first." Valdar's demeanor changed as he ran fingertips down a screen and the mute icons disappeared.

Hoffman felt small next to the shorter admiral. Valdar had a command presence that few could match.

"Dotari First Tier," he said, "time is of the essence, so I'll skip the pleasantries. There is a cloud of moon debris between the Crucible and Syracuse Prime. It's held together by an artificial gravity field about which we have a limited understanding, but we know enough to leverage this to the next phase of operations. The Kesaht have a fleet with five times as many ships as our combined strength in low orbit."

Egan flicked a hand in the holo tank and the image changed to the planet. Knots of red icons appeared on one side of the planet, opposite the main cities on Syracuse's largest continent.

"The Syracuse system's macro cannons dealt the Kesaht armada a blow they won't forget, but enough of their ships survived to establish low orbit anchorage over the southern continent. The outer system macro cannons can't fire on the Kesaht, as any miss would lead to massive damage to the planet."

"What is the issue with shooting dirt?" a Dotari officer asked.

"Macro cannons are brute-force weapons," Egan said. "Brute force at significant speed. Macro cannon shells would hit with enough force to cause an ecological disaster. We don't want to destroy Syracuse to save it."

"The Kesaht landed ground forces and are pushing on the planet's rail batteries." Valdar touched the holo and a ring of emplacements formed around the main city. "If they take even two or three, their fleet can maneuver through the city without significant casualties. That would be the end of the colony. Kesaht have bombarded more than one city from orbit in this conflict." The admiral's voice went icy.

"There's a small colony force led by Colonel Heinrich Fallon on the ground," Egan said. "He's said, 'The situation is in doubt.'"

"Fallon?" Hoffman frowned. He knew that name.

A Dotari, a fleet commander with gold braids on both shoulders, clicked his beak several times, then glared at Hoffman. "Send your Strike Marines to defend this southern hemisphere. Take pressure off the colonel and his small force. Perhaps they can redeem themselves for their failure on the Crucible."

Egan leaned close to Hoffman and whispered, "That is Captain Caz'ul's uncle, Admiral Bat'ov. Their family holds multiple positions on the Council of Firsts."

"It can get worse," Hoffman said under his breath.

"Don't worry about it," Egan said quietly as the human and Dotari admirals spoke. "I've yet to go through a military operation that went as planned."

"People are dead," Hoffman said.

"That's war."

Valdar leaned on the table, then drew the holo view out and away from Syracuse. "This fight will be won in the skies. We need to close with and destroy the Kesaht fleet before the ground batteries fall."

"We will be vulnerable on approach to the planet," Bat'ov said.

"There's not much time," Valdar said. "The Kesaht fouled the atmosphere, shutting off most communication with the colony. We haven't contacted the colony proper, just Colonel Fallon's packet."

"Packet?" Bat'ov asked. "That is clever. With the ionosphere ruined, they must be desperate to send out a mutual-aid request. Why did my staff not receive this packet?"

"They detected our wormhole arrival from Koen," Egan said. "The defenders launched a rocket with a beacon that sent the message on the smoke line, a hidden communication channel used by Terran technicians. I didn't expect Dotari would monitor that channel. I am sending each of you the digitized transcription."

The Dotari commander and his staff skimmed over their screens with a lot of excited nods, quill rustling, and beak clicking.

"This is very detailed for a general, unencrypted message. Very reckless," Bat'ov said.

"They're desperate." Egan glanced briefly at Valdar before continuing. "I imagine Colonel Fallon thought the unencrypted nature of the report would be a moot point if all his people were dead. The rocket and its packet was a last-ditch effort."

"So here we are, as humans say," Bat'ov said. "We must assemble the largest possible force to address this threat."

Valdar studied the human and Dotari reactions. "Don't

count on reinforcements soon. The Crucible is off-line while engineers repair it."

"We are lucky to have the Crucible at all," Bat'ov said, "if not for the noble sacrifice of many Dotari lives."

Hoffman remained where he was, sure that his presence was somehow embarrassing Admiral Valdar. He'd almost appreciate a public rebuke if it would help the situation with the Dotari and get the mission briefing back on track. Hoffman had a duty to take one for the team, even if it looked like the Dotari admiral wanted to reach through the holo and punch the lieutenant.

"We will honor those Dotari lives," Valdar said. "Let's focus on what we can do to save future lives. Syracuse Prime is under attack. It's up to us to break the siege and hold what we have until reinforcements arrive."

"None of your Strike Marines died assaulting the Crucible!" hissed Bat'ov. He clicked his beak, then hissed even louder. "You're asking more Dotari to die to save this world."

"Yes," Valdar said evenly. "I am asking that. I requested aid from the Council of Firsts to fight the Kesaht. Was I wrong to do this?"

Bat'ov's beak worked from side to side. "You are Valdar of the *Breitenfeld*," Bat'ov said. "You saved our people from the Xaros on Takeni. You brought the cure for the phage and rescued our Golden Fleet. We cannot repay the debt to you. Ever."

Egan stepped back closer to Hoffman and crossed his arms. "Here it comes...again. Every Dotari I meet, young or old, has been more dramatic since they lifted their ban on courtship and mating."

"TMI," Hoffman muttered quietly.

"I must take word of Caz'ul's death back to my brother," Bat'ov said. "My emotions are raw."

"We will honor his sacrifices once this battle is over," Valdar said.

"Yes, of course. My apologies, Admiral Valdar. We mourn your losses of many human lives. But I do not think even a hero should be spared punishment when they are incompetent." Bat'ov leaned forward accusingly, clicking his beak in a way Hoffman had never seen before.

"I'm not sure where you're going with this," Valdar said, "but I know we don't have time for it."

"No time! I bring you my grievance and you do not have time? Is Lieutenant Hoffman above recriminations for his incompetence? The Council of Firsts will demand an explanation. I must have answers for them."

Hoffman stepped forward and stood at attention. Valdar waved him back. "Admiral Bat'ov, I've been patient. I've been calm. Should you persist with this complaint in this setting, you will see me angry. Now is not the time."

"Sir, I take full responsibility—" Hoffman began.

"That's enough, Lieutenant. If the admiral wishes to discuss your dedication to saving Dotari lives, then we'll do so. But not here, not now." Valdar stared down the admiral.

The only sounds on the bridge were the normally

forgotten creaks of a ship in the void and soft chimes from a few of the computer workstations.

Valdar activated a tactical display for his audience to see. "Let's move on. Kesaht claw ships and corvettes are spreading through the system, hunting for the macro cannon emplacements."

"How long until the macro cannons are eliminated?" Bat'ov asked.

"Days." Valdar didn't need to look at his notes or the display he had put up for the Dotari captains to see. "Once they nullify the system macro canons, the ships can move out to high orbit and bombard the planet—which was the first thing they did when they arrived in system, before the macros could lock in on them. The smaller ships have a head start on us. We could run them down if I disperse our fleets, but we won't have enough time to save the rail batteries on the planet."

"The problem we're having is right here." A portion of the space field magnified to show a wing of the Kesaht armada. "This battle group is one and a half times our total strength. It's moved away from the main fleet and will be coming for us once the planet rotates enough to keep their interdiction fleet safe from rail guns on the surface. The ships are small and maneuverable enough that engaging them with the system's macro cannons is a waste of time. Plus, it would flag the macro cannon locations. Not every macro fired during the initial invasion, so the question of how many more there are is probably putting some doubt in the Kesaht commander's mind."

Hoffman hung on the admiral's every word. None of the

Dotari interrupted him this time.

"We're going to intercept the Kesaht fleet *inside* the shattered moon, then launch the fleet's Dotari Armor complement to the planet and reinforce the ground battle. Then we'll work out a plan to blow the Kesaht out of Syracuse's skies. My executive officer is sending out movement coordinates and required timelines. It's critical we keep the shattered moon between them and the planet to screen from any long-range Kesaht attacks. Follow these orders to the letter, and discuss any questions or problems you have with my XO. Every ship has its part to play. Every one of you is important to drawing the Kesaht into the position required for our victory. *Gott mit uns.*"

Hoffman watched in quiet amazement as the Dotari admiral and his captains acquiesced without further argument. They'd been quarrelsome, but when it came time for battle, they trusted Valdar implicitly.

"Cod mittens," Bat'ov said and vanished from the holo.

One by one, the rest of the holograms blinked off and Valdar turned and stared at Hoffman. "Egan, give me a moment with the lieutenant."

"Aye, aye," Egan said, retreating to his workstation to confirm and send the fleet orders.

"Thomas," Valdar said, "I appreciate your willingness to take one for the team. But I'll decide when or if I'm willing to let another admiral chastise any of my people."

"Yes, sir." Hoffman felt heat rushing to his face. He was more comfortable with the admiral than when they first met, but this man was still a legend. He wished he'd done a better job, not just to save lives and spare the *Breitenfeld* critical damage, but to stand tall in the admiral's eyes.

"Egan may have already told you, but Caz'ul was a son of a Dotari Council of Firsts member. And not just any member, but a Tier One."

"I'm not sure what that means," Hoffman said, instantly feeling like an idiot for interrupting.

"It's their equivalent of a senior senator—a Dotari with enough power to end the admiral's career and the careers of all his captains," Valdar said. "The captains are concerned. This type of thing makes them all look bad, no matter whose fault it is, even if it's no body's fault."

"The Crucible assault briefing went poorly. I put forth the suggestion we combine our forces and secure the area before continuing to—"

Valdar waved a hand. "Friction. The fog of war. It happens in combat. If you haven't figured out by now that I'm not holding you accountable for this one, then I don't know what to tell you. I've been working with the Dotari long enough to understand them I'll smooth it over. You may have some difficulty in the future in the way of tough questions. Gut it out."

"Yes, sir."

"The Dotari owed me enough favors to send their QRF battlegroup with me to save human colonies. I can handle them, even when their daddies are big shots." He brought up a holograph of the shattered moon. "You did your job and they should be counting their blessings you arrived at the control node when you did. They can't have your head on a silver platter. I need you for the next mission."

"Of course, sir. Thank you, sir."

"This next part will be tricky, but here's what I need you to do…"

****

"What a shit show," Garrison said, dropping his gear to the deck of the *Breitenfeld*'s Marine equipment bay. He peeled off his pseudo-muscle layer to the waist and leaned both hands on his locker. "I'm revising my opinion of the Dotari."

King, sitting on a bench, his elbows on his knees and his attention between his feet, heard the breacher and said nothing. Hearing the normally cocky, sarcastic corporal sound defeated upset King further.

"We can do a more thorough after-action review later," King said. "Need to get our gear turned around for the next mission. Anyone know when that'll be?" he asked, raising his voice so the rest of the Marines in the bay heard him.

"Any damn minute," they said as one.

"Garrison, go through your armor's body cam and note your breach times. I know you were operating faster than textbook standards, but we need to get all that information back to the Corps on Earth. See if there's a better way to breach a Crucible."

"I could've been faster," Garrison said. "Don't think we

90

need a powwow to know where that mission got goat-screwed. Name one human that could've done better, and I'll buy you a bottle of Standish's Finest."

"Such humility," Booker said, shaking her head.

Garrison ignored her. "I need to drop all my gear in the sonic cleanser. Freaking blood everywhere."

Max shrugged. "At least it's not mine this time. Most of this belongs to the Rakka."

For the first time in his career, King just glared at them, too tired to chew their collective asses.

"Are you trying to cheer me up?" Garrison asked. "We go through hell and the Dotari are all up in our ass when it was their stupid captain's plan that botched everything."

"Every mission is like that," King said. "We're expected to adapt and overcome. No excuses."

"Tell *them* that," Garrison said as he grabbed all his gear and walked into the sonic shower.

"I agree," Booker said to Max, giving him a sidelong look as she pulled off a pauldron. "Least none of this is human blood. You want to get blood on your hands, try being a medic."

"You want me to apologize for bleeding all over you?" Max lifted an arm, exposing a long, pink scar on his midriff.

"That even healed?" Duke asked, spitting a dab of tobacco into a water bottle.

"I held my own in that fight, thank you very much." Max removed a boot and flexed his foot.

"Gunney," Duke said, tilting his head to the door, "we got

time for me to make a foundry run? I need an upgrade."

"You need a shower?" King asked.

Duke sniffed his armpit, paused, then sniffed a second time and shook his head.

"Go," King said as Max and Booker carried their gear into the showers.

King stayed where he was, rear on the bench and elbows on his knees, thinking about his career and all the things he'd seen before this mission. His team's bickering was almost soothing. The voices had a peculiar sound as they echoed from the shower. The sonic cleaning was nearly silent, but still distorted the words. He could see them but wasn't actively watching their argument.

Opal sat on another bench across from King, as still as if in a reverie, his heavy gauss rifle half assembled, a mud-and-grease-stained rag in one of his mottled green-and-brown hands.

"Hey, Gunney," Garrison asked as he came out of the shower, the chest and back armor he carried emanating steam, "has Opal just been standing there the whole time?"

Booker dropped her armor and rushed to the doughboy who was still as a statue staring at the wall. She snapped her fingers in front of his face. "Hey there, big guy…why isn't he breathing?"

Booker put her palm to Opal's chest then all the color drained from her face.

"He's ice cold. System's shutting down. Garrison, my pack. Now!"

Garrison grabbed Booker's medic bag and tossed it to her. She dropped to one knee and unzipped a pouch reserved just for

Opal. Using a special injector designed for doughboys, she plucked the cap off the stimulant and tapped the end against the battle construct's thigh.

"These things aren't easy to come by," she said. "Max, go get Hoffman."

Max backed away. "What's that going to do to him?"

"Go. Get. Hoffman."

Max backed toward the door, worry writ across his face. He stopped half in and half out of the locker room.

She stabbed the stim into Opal's thigh and there was a pneumatic hiss. Opal's eyes dilated and he took in a deep breath. His face ticked from one side to the other, then he looked down at the stim embedded in his thigh.

"Unit functioning," Opal said and Booker pulled the stim and it's three inch long needle out of Opal's leg.

King came to stand beside Booker. "He's been acting weird. Everyone except Booker, step back in case he flips out. Doughboys can get twitchy when they degr—whatever's happening to him."

Garrison grabbed Opal's right arm at the elbow and wrist, a classic setup for a restraint hold. "No way, Gunney. Opie's not gonna crash on us. We gotta help him."

King grabbed the other arm, even though he doubted they could hold the doughboy for even a second if he went into a rage.

"Do it."

"This is gonna sting, big guy." Booker jabbed the injector into Opal's thigh. There was a hiss, but no reaction from Opal.

"Huh, that's funny." The medic looked down at the injector and pulled it from Opal's flesh.

"Did it work?" Garrison tightened his hold on Opal.

"Reads empty." Booker looked Opal in the eye and put the pad of her thumb against his neck. "Respiration's returned to normal. Heart rate's steady. I'm taking his blood pressure now and it's normal."

"Why hasn't Max brought the lieutenant?" King asked.

"Because it's only been about ninety seconds," Duke said. "And I can still hear him beating feet down the passageway."

Opal shuddered like a wet dog shaking his fur as the Strike Marines kept his arms pinned to his side. Opal looked up, his eyes dilated.

"Opal…hungry."

"Good job, Opie," Booker said. "Really good job."

Opal looked at her questioningly, then frowned. "Opal. Hungry. Feed Opal."

"Yeah, sure thing, big guy," Garrison said. "I've got some whey protein bars. You like strawberry, yeah?"

"Red ones," Opal said as he began reassembling his weapon.

"Poggie bait OK for him right now?" King asked Booker.

"Doughboys don't react to meds and food like us," she said. "He should be fine. *Should.* We need to get him to a specialist back on Earth. The lieutenant's had a lot more experience with him than me. He'd know if Opal's about to…you know."

Shut down, King thought. The vast majority of doughboys

94

had broken down shortly after the Ember War. Opal and a few others kept functioning, though no one had been able to explain why.

There were a few things in Hoffman's past that the lieutenant didn't care to speak of, and the loss of his doughboy platoon was one of them. King knew he had a difficult conversation with his team leader coming up soon.

"Here you go, Opal." Garrison tossed a foil-wrapped bar to the doughboy. Opal caught it and ate it in two bites, not bothering to unwrap it.

"Why does he always eat like that?" Booker asked.

"Taste better," Opal said, his jaw working.

"Chow run," King said. "Bring a tray back for Opal."

"You don't want us to—" Garrison ceased his objection as King gave him a stern look.

Opal kept working on his weapon as the other Marines left. King watched the doughboy work, his hands moving same as ever, following the precise program to clean and reassemble it.

"Opal, run diagnostic routine nine-delta, authorization King one-one."

Opal's back straightened and an eye twitched. "Unit functioning within parameters," Opal said. He raised one hand and knocked his rifle to the deck. Opal paused for a moment, then picked it up and went back to work.

"No you're not, big guy," King said. "No you're not."

****

Duke sat on a low bench, tapping his foot, and crossing and uncrossing his arms. Sailors moved from the main hallway, shuttling parts and equipment from the *Breitenfeld's* 3D printing foundries.

The door he was watching slid open. A tall, thin man who looked like a scientist with faded, nonmilitary tattoos leaned out. "You might as well come inside. I'm nearly finished," Walther, the foundry tech, said from the door, his hands still gloved.

Duke jumped to his feet, entered, and marched toward the workbench.

"Have a seat, Sergeant," the tech said.

Duke found a new place to sit where he began fidgeting worse than he had in the waiting room.

The technician returned to his station and studied his work through goggles as he held tools fit for a surgeon in his rubber-gloved hands. Lights shined down from the goggles—sometimes dim, sometimes bright, and sometimes pulsing a low-intensity laser to get exact measurements. Seconds passed between his movements; the only sounds in the room were the ventilation and Duke tapping his foot.

Without looking up, the technician said, "You're antsy for a sniper. Pretend you're on a mission or something."

Duke's foot stopped. Three seconds later, it started again.

"I was pretty nervous when my first son was born. Probably drove my wife crazy pacing the obstetrics ward. It got easier after the third kid." He frowned at something Duke couldn't see, then spoke again without looking up. "It's been a few years."

Duke leaned forward, planted his elbows on his knees, and violently rubbed his face and buzz-cut hair. "Are you about done?"

"You want me to rush this? Your specifications on the capacitor settings were way out of standard tolerances."

"No. Take your time." He stood. "Have you ever lost part of your body?"

"Ah, ah, ah. You know the rules. No peeky, peeky. I'll send you outside again." He lowered his voice, speaking almost to himself. "You know the docs can regrow a limb easy enough these days. What you want...that's something special."

"Let me help. I know precision rifles inside and out."

"Speak less than thou knowest."

Duke frowned. "Shakespeare?"

The tattooed technician nodded gravely as the nearby foundry began to construct something huge. Duke noticed the subtle changes—the vibrating walls, the slight change in air pressure.

"You're the strangest, most aggravating gunsmith I've ever met."

"I'm not a gunsmith. I'm an omnium foundry tech...but the best omni printer you'll ever meet," the technician said, pausing, then moving a lighted camera to examine the interior of the barrel. "I heard you were the best at what you do—which makes me glad you're on our side. The most finely crafted precision gauss rifle ever made with the most advanced technology available to humankind, in the hands of the legend of Koensuu

City."

Duke sat, leaned back against the bulkhead, and closed his eyes. Time crawled as the technician went over every piece of the weapon with scientific thoroughness. Lines from *King Lear* ran through his head.

"Finished."

Duke strode to the table and looked down at a twin-vane rail rifle. The receiver was shiny, the vanes reflecting light like mirrors.

"It looks so…plain."

"Everything special's on the inside." The man stood back, arms crossed, smiling arrogantly.

Duke checked to make sure it wasn't loaded, then pointed it into the corner. He looked down iron sights with his right eye but kept both eyes open, then pulled the three-stage trigger one stage at a time.

"Your scope's printing." The technician went to an assembly unit built into a wall where servo arms whirled within a cabinet.

Duke held the weapon away from his body, studying it from ninety degrees. His eyes traveled from the end of the barrel to the stock and back again, then he lifted it a bit higher and slammed it on the ground.

Walther yelled and backed against the wall as Duke stood on it and hopped up and down.

"What…what the hell are you doing!"

Ignoring the technician, Duke picked up the rifle and did a

quick functions check. When that was completed, he turned the optics on. "Now I run the diagnostics."

Using one hand to steady himself, the technician walked along the wall to the bench and sat down. "I can't believe that just happened. I just…I mean I knew Strike Marines were crazy, but…the horror."

"I don't want to find out you put her together wrong while I'm in the field," Duke said.

"I'm insulted." Walther's face contorted with anger.

"And I'd be pretty dead if you botched the job, but she checks out." Duke went to a workbench and pawed through tools until he found an engraver. "Here we go."

Carefully and with less artistry than the *Breitenfeld* gunsmith, he engraved *Ice Claw* on the stock.

"What have you done!"

"She's no Buffy, but she'll do."

"Get out of my workshop. You can't take something as perfectly balanced—"

Duke stepped close, practically breathing the man's air. In a low, gravelly voice he might use after hours watching a target, he said, "What do you think I'm going to do with this rifle? I'll never drop her or mistreat her. I'll throat punch anyone who touches her. But sooner or later, I'm going to get smashed across an alien death ship by some freak of the galaxy no one's ever seen and my rifle better be ready when I stand up to kill the unlucky bastard who did it."

The technician swallowed hard. "That makes sense. I will

factor that into my next design."

Duke smiled and nodded as he studied the rifle, then patted the technician on the shoulder. "Good work, old man. You can use my name as an endorsement if you ever go into business for yourself. The White Fate endorses this rifle."

****

Duke slid his foot into a sabaton and slapped the calf. It tightened around his foot with a hiss and he lifted it off the deck. Magnetic and anti-grav plates flickered on and off as his power armor ran through a diagnostic.

"Damn mag locks are on the fritz again." He put his foot on a bench and picked up a gauntlet with a screen built into it.

"Why didn't you grab some spares while you were in the foundry?" Booker asked as she attached leg armor to the pseudo-muscle layer over her quads.

"I didn't know these had crapped out, did I? I *needed* a new rail rifle," Duke said.

"Overcompensating?" Garrison said with a snicker as he pulled his armor out of a locker cage.

"Yeah, for your shit aim." Duke spat tobacco juice into a water bottle.

"Put a bigger optic on your new toy. Your vision's going in your old age," Garrison said.

"I'm still surprised you survived childhood." Duke kicked

the bench with his malfunctioning boot and a high-pitched whine filled the locker room. "There. I fixed it."

Max, sitting half out of his power armor across from Duke, was fixated on a data slate, tapping away.

"None of you dickheads sent a message home about me being hit, right?" he asked. "*Mamasita* hears about my flesh wound through the grape vine, she'll lose her damn mind."

"Your medevac order's in the system," Booker said. "That should generate a message through channels back to the rear detachment. I don't remember if the lieutenant sent anything to Earth. The situation was pretty fluid on Koen."

"By 'fluid' do you mean balls-freezing cold?" Garrison asked. "By the Saint I hate that planet. Ice. Wolves. Ibarran spies mocking me with their flirty gaze just to taze my ass and throw me in a cell. Spies! Can't trust them."

"Boo-God-damn-hoo," Max smirked. "Your peanuts got frost-burnt. I needed three pints of blood."

"Remember to duck next time, dingleberry." Garrison took out his multi-tool for breaching and gave it kiss before he locked it onto his armor.

Max's data slate pinged. "Priority alert from Gunney," he said.

"I'm not dressed yet," Duke said, putting on his other sabaton.

"Mission clock hasn't changed…we're getting a new team member," Max said.

The Strike Marines looked over to Adams' locker, still full

of her gear.

"Now?" Garrison asked. "We got some rookie from Quantico already? Where was this shirker during the fight on the Crucible? What the hell kind of a Strike Marine sits out—"

"It's a Dotari advisor," Max said and the Marines groaned.

"It's not that winner what's-his-face, is it?" Booker asked. "Lothar? He was a damn potato in a fight."

"Gunney didn't say." Max shrugged. "Just ordered us to get Adams' power armor and set it to factory default so we can fit it to a Dotari."

"That's bad luck," Duke said. "You can't zero out a Marine's armor unless they're...not coming back."

"Guess that tells us something about Adams." Max went to the absent Marine's locker and pulled out her breastplate. Reaching underneath, he squeezed a switch for a few seconds and the suit of pseudo muscles inside loosened slowly.

"We need to dress up a Dotari like us so they don't stand out like a please-shoot-me-sore-thumb on the battlefield," Garrison said. "Doesn't mean anything about Adams."

"I think it's time we accepted that she's just not coming back," Booker said. "Not a damn peep about her since she was reassigned out of the blue. Nothing. Maybe she got picked up for some black-ops job. Body guard for President Garret or something."

"Wait," Garrison said, putting his hands on his hips, "Hoffman said that Ibarran spy, Masha, was talking about Adams. Like she knew something about her."

"Just a mind game," Duke said. "Worked pretty well. She and her knuckle dragger got away."

"Thanks, dick," Max said to Garrison and pointed to the scar Medvedev's bullet gave him.

"We got jumped from behind," Garrison said, throwing his hands up, "by *cops* of all people."

Booker reached into Adams' locker and stretched out the power armor's under suit. "Adams was part of this team. Don't you think we should know what happened to her?"

"You care? Now you're the team princess," Duke said.

"Have I got an ounce of slack since she was gone?" Booker asked. "Ass. What if it was you that up and vanished?"

"They'd have to decommission the team. You'd be combat ineffective without me."

Booker stretched out the legs of the inner suit, smoothing the pseudo muscles that kept Adam's shape.

"Duke, you're old as hell. Have you ever seen someone removed from a team like this?"

All eyes fell on the sniper.

He shook his head. "No. Not like this."

"So what are we going to do about it?" she asked.

No one spoke.

"You assholes are the best team I've ever been part of," she said. "She was part of that team. She's our sister and if she's in trouble, we have a duty to help her."

"I'm not worried," Garrison said.

"You're full of crap," Booker said.

"I second that," Max added.

Duke squared off to Booker, pointing a finger at her. "One of us has to talk to the boss, and I think that person should be you."

"Not so fun now, is it?" Garrison said.

"Maybe I should ask Gunney," she said.

"That'll go well," Duke said. "Take my advice. This is something only the L-T can fix. If it can be fixed. Leave it alone. If he knew something, he'd tell us."

"If he knew something and was allowed to tell us, he'd tell us," Max corrected.

Duke spat into his bottle flecked with tobacco leaves. "Yeah, you're right, Max."

"Everyone get your shit on and get prepped," Max said. "Gunney comes in here and catches us in the middle of a pity party, we'll wish we were with Adams. Wherever the hell she is."

****

Deep within the *Breitenfeld*, Hoffman checked the number on a door. This part of the ship was a warren of narrow passageways and offices away from the near chaos of the rest of the ship. He was reaching up to knock on the door when it slid open.

A naval commander in alert dress—a jumpsuit over a void skin suit that could be made vacuum ready in a few seconds by donning gloves and a helmet—stood in the doorway.

"Lieutenant Hoffman," the commander said. His name tape read CHRISTIE. "You're late."

"Apologies, sir. This ship has an older layout. Every time I thought I had the right passageway it led to a dead end," he said.

"The *Breit* was a training ship until a few months ago, not exactly optimized. Come in." Christie motioned to the room behind him where two chairs faced each other and a desk was pushed against the bulkhead. Christie had it set up for an interrogation.

Hoffman looked around the room as he took a seat, noting several small camera domes.

"Am I going to be under oath?" Hoffman asked.

"Smart. Who told you I was intelligence?" Christie sat and removed a metal band from a shoulder pocket.

"You've got the furniture arrayed so you can see my feet— the better to monitor my body language—and multi-spectrum cameras to monitor my heart rate, respiration and skin temperature…sir."

"Then there's no need to put you under oath, is there? I'll know if you're lying. ' Christie put the band over the top of his head and flipped down a small screen over one eye.

"This ship's heading to another battle. Your time is better spent prepping for that, so let's get down to brass tacks, yes?" the intelligence officer asked.

"I appreciate that. I haven't had the chance to do a post-operation write-up of the mission to seize the Crucible, but—"

"You got a prominent Dotari captain killed. Despite all

that the Terran Union's done for the Dotari, they're still aliens—aliens with different notions of right and wrong. Our alliance with them is crucial, in case you haven't noticed. This fleet is Syracuse's only chance of surviving, and only one ship is Union. All the armor is Dotari," Christie said.

"I'm not a politician," Hoffman said, regretting the words immediately.

"And we don't expect you to be. Pre-Ember War Strike Marines had the old foreign internal defense mission. Drop behind enemy lines and recruit a force to disrupt an enemy state. Something Green Berets did before the Atlantic Union reorganization," the intelligence officer said.

"Are you waxing on while your sensors get a biometric baseline for my reactions? Just skip to the hard questions, sir."

"I see why Valdar likes you," Christie smirked. "No time for bullshit. Must remind him of Ken Hale. He does miss his godson."

"You mentioned brass tacks."

"Why did Captain Caz'ul die?"

"Other than the Kesaht bullets? The plan called for my team to drop on the access corridor between the hangar and the control center. I've looked back over the recon data. The Kesaht changed the Crucible's configuration on our approach and the plan didn't adjust accordingly. My team did the best we could in a fluid situation."

"You're blaming Caz'ul?"

"Battlefields are fluid. You know so much about the pre–

Atlantic Union militaries. Didn't they have a saying about how no plan survives first contact with the enemy? Strike Marines are still trained to adapt and overcome."

"Our Dotari allies are a bit more rigid…" Christie trailed off, watching Hoffman.

The lieutenant held his posture and didn't give any external sign that Christie's giving him some benefit of the doubt had offered him some relief.

"And the admiral explained that much to them," the intelligence officer continued. "Even after working side by side with the Dotties for years, there are still frustrations. They're mature enough to recognize them and Valdar has a never-ending supply of trump cards and silver bullets to use on them. He is Valdar. This is the *Breitenfeld*. You think Noah's descendants argued with the guy that built the ark?"

"You've lost me."

"Sorry. Waxing again," he said with a wink. "I have to ask about Gor'al as there are some other elements that cast doubt on you."

Hoffman's face flushed with anger and he didn't care if Christie could see it.

"What 'doubt'?" Hoffman asked, with anger on the edge of his voice.

"Things I'd ignore if the Keystone wasn't aboard. That piece of technology is critical to the Terran Union. The only mobile gate in existence with an extended jump distance. Crucial to the Union's long-term strategy in the war against the Kesaht. I wish

Valdar had returned it to Earth before this mission, but the admiral isn't one to risk lives for the sake of technology."

"What about the Keystone?"

"Your team captured a pair of Ibarran spies…then they escaped."

"Because of sleeper agents on Koen. Not because we let them go," Hoffman said. "You know what we went through to track them down? We chased Masha and Medvedev across four different planets before we ran them down. If the Kesaht hadn't been about to overrun the city, my entire—"

Christie held up a hand. "I read your report. Everything passes the smell test. Everything except Corporal Adams."

Hoffman's brows rose. "Adams? What does she have to do with this?"

"Maybe nothing. Maybe everything. You're aware that she's a procedural human being. One of the last to come out of the tanks after the Hale Treaty was signed."

"No," Hoffman frowned. "The Naissance Act is pretty clear that it doesn't matter how anyone is born. It's incredibly illegal to even search records for that information. Hell, I'm a procedural." He touched his face. "I had plastic surgery in the tank to come out looking like Jared Hale so the doughboys would imprint on me easier. What about Adams? Do you know where she is?"

"I know where she *was*. She was on Mars, locked up with other procedurals suspected of being Ibarran sleeper agents."

"No. She couldn't be. She's loyal to the Union and the

Corps." Hoffman stood up and took a step to the door.

"Sit down," Christie said, an edge to his voice that gave Hoffman pause. "You don't understand Marc and Stacey Ibarra. Before they turned traitor and ran off with the 13th Fleet, they succeeded in planting command protocols in a number of procedurals. Adams was one of them. You may not like it but when someone controls the mind that goes into your body, it's not like she could have acted of her own free will."

"You're lying," Hoffman said, but he sat back down, resting his elbows on his lap.

"Take a look." Christie removed a data slate from a hip pocket and passed it to the lieutenant. Video feed from inside a prison played out. Men and women in orange jumpsuits fought black-armored Rangers and Hoffman recognized Adams right away. She held a captured gauss carbine the way he remembered and moved with a Strike Marine's finesse.

When she shot down Rangers, Hoffman's jaw fell open. "No...it can't be."

"A team of Ibarran operatives infiltrated the prison and triggered the sleeper-agent protocols. They escaped, killing several dozen guards in the process, and they got away with a number of our armor soldiers that had...been detained."

"How the hell could Ibarrans get onto Mars and—wait. Wait. Who were the operatives?" Hoffman asked.

Christie touched a small screen mounted on his wrist. The data slate brought up two pictures: Medvedev in crew overalls inside a hangar and Masha in a flight suit.

"God damn it!" Hoffman threw the slate against the bulkhead.

"A lot of that going around," Christie smirked.

Hoffman stood and faced away from the intelligence officer, his hands on his hips, his chin low.

"So you can appreciate why there's doubt," Christie said. "A pair of Ibarran agents slipped out of your grasp. Those same spies then engineered a prison break aided by one of your Marines. Lots of questions about that incident lead back to you, Hoffman."

"What do you want from me?" the lieutenant asked. "Adams was a good Marine every moment I knew her. She thought the Ibarrans were traitors. She never tried to turn me or my team to their side, if that's what you're getting at."

"That is what I'm getting at." Christie tapped the eyepiece. "But your reactions are consistent with someone telling the truth. So let's end this line of questioning." He reached under his seat and pulled out a gauss pistol.

"What the hell?" Hoffman asked, his feet planted firmly on the deck.

"Guillotine," Christie said, his eyes locked on the lieutenant. "Tecumseh. Geranium. Circus."

"I know you intel types can be squirrely, but have you gone nuts?" Hoffman asked.

"I didn't think so." The spy put the gun back under the seat. "You're on our side. Surprise. Don't say those words in that order to anyone else, understand?"

"That's how the Ibarrans activated their sleeper agents."

Hoffman crossed his arms over his chest.

"Sharp for Marine. That'll do it for us, Lieutenant. This entire conversation is classified. You breathe a word of it and you'll be peeling potatoes in some shit-hole colony for the rest of your days. Doesn't matter who's taken a liking to you."

"Heard. I'll be going."

"Just one more thing…" Christie wagged a finger in the air.

"Really, sir?"

"You're getting a new team member at the Dotari's instance. Gor'al. He's their local expert on human culture and will be your liaison so we don't have another debacle like we had on the Crucible. I'll debrief you once he's transferred back to their fleet."

Hoffman pinched the bridge of his nose. "Not another Dotari on my team…"

"Valdar's idea." Christie shrugged.

The screen on Hoffman's forearm beeped. He glanced at a text message and ran out the door.

"Mouth shut!" Christie called after him.

****

Hoffman looked around a cargo container and saw nothing but dusty boxes. He hurried down the next row and found Gunney King standing next to Opal. The doughboy stood. Wires from an open box on the floor connected to Opal's head and bare torso.

"Opie?" Hoffman ran up to the doughboy and snapped his fingers on either side of his face. Opal's head snapped from side to side, looking at the source of the noise.

"I couldn't take him to sick bay," King said. "They're still treating wounded from the last fight and they sure as hell don't know what to do with him. I got one of the foundry techs to assemble a diagnostic unit. Thank God they still have the plans on file."

"He stopped breathing?" Hoffman went to the open box and swiped through menus on the screen.

"Looks like. Booker gave him a shot of go juice and he's been normal since." King stepped back.

"Battle constructs have hyper-oxygenated fluid in place of blood," Hoffman said. "They can go ten minutes without air before they—Opal, fluctuate your right lung. Subroutine sigma sigma seven."

Air sucked into a single nostril and Opal exhaled unevenly.

"You see the new personnel assignment?" King asked.

"I heard it through the grapevine." Hoffman stood up and rapped his knuckles on Opal's chest with slight force.

"Sir, I don't know exactly what you're doing and I'm not sure I'm value-added to this equation," King said.

"I got it. Get the team set." Hoffman rubbed a hand down his face.

"You all right?" King asked.

"It's just one damn thing after another," the lieutenant said. "But we don't quit in the Strike Marine Corps. We'll catch up.

I need to run a few more tests on Opal."

"Roger." King patted Hoffman's shoulder as he left.

"Sir…hurt?" Opal grumbled.

"No, Opie…" Hoffman leaned back against the containers across from the coughboy. "You feeling good?"

"Diamond 9-9 went dark," Opal said.

"He did. Years ago. The whole platoon went dark, but not you, Opal. You're tougher than that. You're tougher than all of them. Can you be tougher?"

"Yes, sir."

"Ah…" Hoffman sank down, resting his arms on his knees. "You remember the old me? How I used to look?"

"You are you. Your face changed. Still you."

"Soon as you all started going dark, the brigade let us go back to our original look. No need to be Jared Hale if there were no doughboys to follow us. Most of the others were glad to change—helped get over the loss of you all. New start on life…I wonder if I should've kept that face. Kept true to you and your brothers."

"You are you."

"I'm a screwup, is what I am. You wouldn't believe what I just found out. I am ate up. You know that? Everything we've done keeps turning to crap. Maybe we should've taken a colony assignment. You and me, Opal. Working the farm. Maybe own a bar. You'd be a crap bouncer as you can't harm a single human being."

"Dotties," Opal said.

"What? Oh…them. Every single 'attaboy' can get erased by a single 'oh crap,' you know that?"

"Dotty baby."

"Huh. Lo'thar's little girl." Hoffman let out a slow breath. "Guess she'll be all right, thanks to us. Can't take that away."

"I won't go dark," Opal said. "Sir needs me."

"I do, Opal…I do." Hoffman stood and detached the wires from the doughboy's mottled flesh. "You ready for another fight?"

"Kill Kesaht." His hands balled into fists.

"That's my boy. Chance to crack some skulls and you perk right up. We need—"

Opal swung his meaty arms around Hoffman and hugged him against his chest.

"Sir no hurt," Opal grumbled.

"Opie—" Hoffman slapped at the arms squeezing around his neck and shoulders. "Too tight! Too tight!"

Opal released his lieutenant and Hoffman, lightheaded, took in a breath.

"Where enemy?" Opal asked.

"Follow me." Hoffman's shoulder bounced off the side of a cargo container as he stumbled away.

Chapter 8

Hoffman rolled his shoulders, adjusting his armor. His suit had a bad tendency to pinch behind his neck every time he put it on. The pseudo-muscle layer adjusted to the wearer and such discomfort faded away after the bodysuit was properly broken in, but there was still an uncomfortable period. He'd heard armor would stay inside their pods for weeks and months at a time. If Strike Marine power armor could overcome a number of personal hygiene issues, he just might do the same.

His team sat in a Mule, ready but uneasy. Garrison kept glancing at the upper turret, manned by a naval rating. Duke leaned back against his seat, somehow able to sleep.

"Sir," Max said, "we're really going to a Dotty ship?"

"That's right," Hoffman said.

"They weren't exactly happy with us the last time we saw them," the commo tech said.

"Dotties aren't into honor duels or vendettas…I hope." Garrison shifted in his seat. "Did anyone check on that before we got assigned to them?"

"That situation's been dealt with," Hoffman said.

"We got a Dotty babysitter." Booker shook a fist next to her face. "Make sure us hairy apes don't throw our poop all over the place."

"I got some coffee beans," Max said, slapping a pouch on his thigh. "They like those, right? Maybe we can trade it for some of their pogie bait. Or use it for ransom."

"Can I get some of that?" Garrison asked.

"Nope," Max said with a quick shake of his head.

The pilot's voice came over the intercom. *"Thank you for flying Certain Death Space Transports, where my jokes are the last thing you'll ever hear. If you had windows, you'd be able to see, several thousand kilometers to your right, a massive alien fleet intent upon destroying us. Also visible in this delightful space scape is what used to be a moon that was somehow broken apart and then stopped from plummeting into the gravity well of Syracuse Prime, where it would have wiped out all life. You can thank the Xaros Corps of Engineers for that one. Please be sure your tactical displays and deadly weapons are secured and in an upright position. Remain in your seats until we've come to a complete stop on the flight deck of the...*Pure Strike *and always remember to tip your flight attendants... if there were any."*

"Listen to this joker," Garrison said just before the Mule landed on the flight deck of the Dotari frigate without a bump.

"Nice landing," Booker said, gathering her weapons and medical gear.

Hoffman's thoughts went to the perfect landing on the surface of the Crucible before the disastrous Dotari mission. He was proud of his team, but the loss of Dotari lives made him sick to his stomach. Images of bodies blasted apart and savaged by the Kesaht space barbarians threatened to distract him from his current mission.

"Double-check your load-out and double-check your buddy's load-out," King said as he inspected each of the team members stepping off the Mule and onto the flight deck of the *Pure Strike*.

Hoffman looked over Opal and the doughboy returned the favor. The mottle-faced giant was barely smart enough to function, but probably knew Hoffman's gear better than he did. When it came to military activities, Opal's mind was a steel trap—zero defects.

"Sir is ready sir.'

"Thanks, Opal. You're good to go." Hoffman patted him on the arm and went to meet the Dotari officers. Long ago, when he was newly assigned to the doughboy units, he expected them to smile when praised, but they rarely did. Opal was no exception.

None of Hoffman's team commented on the elaborate style of the Dotari landing bay. The ceilings were higher than seemed strictly necessary, as were the arched doorways, and words in the Dotari language scrolled around the borders of both exits. The lighting was modulated to complement the architectural expression of the ship's interior.

Moving away from the flight line, they found a place to put down ready bags and other gear attached to their armor. King checked everyone's vitals with simple questions and a watchful eye.

Booker opened up her medical bag and jotted something

on her data slate.

"Is there a problem?" Hoffman asked.

She shook her head and continued to make notes on the tablet screen. "I always think of things when we're en route. This is one of those rare chances I get to double-check and make sure I have everything."

"Do you have everything?" Hoffman asked.

"Mostly," she said.

Max stretched his arms above his head and then out to the side. "Okay, I'll be the one to say it. This feels a lot like *Kid'ran's Gift*."

"You're right, but this one's full of nice Dotari instead of the mutated, reprogrammed variety wanting to murder us," Garrison said.

Hoffman wasn't sure he would consider the crew of the *Pure Strike* "nice." No one greeted them and a half-dozen members of the maintenance crew simply stared at them.

Undeterred, Garrison strode toward the group with a wave and a smile. "Can one of you fine gentlemen point me to the head?"

The Dotari glanced at his fellows, then pointed his fingers to his temples.

"No no." Garrison rolled his eyes then turned back to the Strike Marines. "Anyone remember how Lo'thar put it? 'Leave one's droppings' or—"

"You are transient." The Dotari cut him off. "Not a guest. It is known among us you allowed Caz'ul to die."

118

Hoffman stepped beside Garrison and put a hand on his arm to stop him from advancing into an argument. The breacher was tense and ready for a fight.

"Just point us to where we're supposed to go," Hoffman said.

The deck workers parted as a Dotari officer approached.

"Lieutenant Hoffman," Gor'al said, touching fingertips to his temple, "welcome to the ship. Different than the *Kidran's Gift*, yes? A bit older. But a friendlier welcome, yes yes?"

"Not quite," Garrison muttered.

"Come, my new jarhead compatriots." Gor'al raised a hand to a doorway across the landing bay. "Our mission awaits."

"I can't wait for this," Duke said. "I really think the brass is pulling our legs."

"Your legs must be used for walking. No bovine leavings. Come come." Gor'al walked off and the team followed.

"Did you volunteer to be our advisor?" Booker asked as she caught up to the Dotari.

"I was ordered to volunteer," Gor'al said. "I've studied human culture and history for so long, it is useful to put that to use."

"You don't seem overly excited," she said.

"Dotari…our culture is changing since the Golden Fleet returned to the home world. There is a renewed interest in our unique culture, what we were before the Alliance and before our time living on Earth during the Ember War. To work so closely with non-Dotari is unpopular in some influential tiers. My family is of that clique."

"Well, we're glad to have you with us," Booker said.

"We are?" Garrison asked. Booker elbowed him in the chest. "We are! Totally! Just that our last advisor didn't know the difference between his ass and a hole in the ground."

Gor'al shifted nervously, looking at each member of the team individually. "I think I know the difference."

"Gor'al is a Marine, not a flyboy. That makes a big difference," Booker said.

"Yes, I am a warrant officer. Flyboys are—how do you say—female cats."

Garrison and the others laughed. "He might work out."

King was less enthusiastic and as he moved forward, the laughter died down. "Where are the entry vehicles?"

Gor'al's enthusiasm returned. He rushed toward the other end of the hangar, waving for them to follow. "Come. This way. I will show you. I think you'll like this very much."

"Did they ever ask your opinion about this plan before they assigned it to us, boss?" Duke asked.

Hoffman shook his head. He had the basics and was starting to realize the details were going to be unpopular with his team. Despite his misgivings, he couldn't deny that Gor'al loved his job and was clearly a huge fan of the Terran Strike Marines.

"This is it. I think you'll be really impressed," Gor'al said as he led them into a munitions bay.

A team of Dotari moved to and from a Tactical Insertion Torpedo, a seventy-foot-long missile nearly ten feet in diameter.

"Wait. What?" Garrison came to sudden stop as he looked over the torpedo. "These are for armor. Not Strike Marines."

Something heavy hit the deck toward the rear of the torpedo and Dotari techs began chattering loudly.

Hoffman glanced at each member of his team, but focused on Duke. The sniper, it was safe to say, was displeased.

Duke's face looked as though he had swallowed some of his chewing tobacco. "No. Not only no, but fu—"

"That's enough of that talk. We're Strike Marines. This is the mission. Salute and execute," King said.

"This is what humans call a really big TIT. It is how we will move into position for the battle," Gor'al said.

"We saw Dotari Armor use these over Koensuu City," Hoffman said. "These pull awfully high g's. Right?"

Gor'al's face all but glowed with admiration. "They are marvels of engineering."

Max snorted. "Armor pilots are protected in their suits—in their pods full of goo. They can withstand high-g maneuvers, sudden stops, things like being spat out of a torp at a thousand miles an hour." He put his fists on his hips. "Thing is, I'm not armor."

"I'm not armor either," Booker said.

"That's why the payload delivery systems are being modified," Gor'al said. "These crash seats have the latest inertial dampening systems."

"Crash seats?" Booker asked with a raised eyebrow.

"They should be called Dynamic Assault Coffins instead,"

Max deadpanned.

Gor'al shook his head vigorously. "No. You must trust me. These are very good. You don't even need to be ejected when we arrive at the insertion point. The sides will retract and the seats will give you a tiny little push away from the TIT as it continues to its final objective," said the Dotari advisor, who seemed surprised by the blank looks this statement earned him.

Opal stood over the torpedo, staring balefully into its interior. "Dark in there."

Hoffman massaged the back of his neck as his team launched a new round of protests and complaints.

"Hey, Max, what do armor pilots call us?" Duke asked.

"Crunchies, I think."

"Squishy," Garrison said.

Max shook his head. "No, I'm pretty sure it's crunchy."

"I was calling you squishy. You're soft," Garrison said, dodging a swing from the commo expert. "Crunchy, squishy...whatever. It's all the same. We get in one of these things, we're pulp on the first high-g turn."

"Don't worry about the turns," Duke said. "Deceleration. That'll kill you. So will acceleration. Basically anything armor does will kill us. Dead. As in you can't come back from getting turned into paste."

"No, no, no. It is very safe. All the computer simulations show a high chance of survival," Gor'al said.

"How high is high? Have you ever rode in one of those things?" Duke asked.

"Not yet!" Gor'al clicked his beak quickly.

"Do Dotari have priests?" Garrison asked. "Could this thing get a blessing?"

"That's enough," King said.

"Yes, Gunney. Shutting down my naturally healthy skepticism...now."

A new group of Dotari technicians entered from a lift large enough to move ship parts...or munitions, a squad of ship security escorting them. Some of the group seemed to be scientists, or maybe engineers. With them was a sled bearing a block of dark metal run through with wire.

Duke spat into a grate off to one side of the work area. "Is that what I think it is?"

Gor'al nodded enthusiastically. "Mark 9 denethrite warhead. It's being added to the payload with us."

Opal grunted and his eyes widened.

"It's all part of the plan," Gor'al said, his quills rustling in a manner that suggested nervousness or embarrassment.

"Hi, friendly neighborhood explosives expert here," Garrison said. "We're going to ride with the warhead? Denethrite is shock-sensitive...just like any bit of boom boom."

"I wasn't going to shoot it for fun," Duke said.

"Shoot it? Don't even fart near it," Garrison said. When more tools fell to the deck behind him, Garrison hunched down.

Duke cursed under his breath. "Did you come up with this plan, Gor'al?"

"No. That is above my place on the List," the Dotari said.

"Walk with me, Gor'al," Hoffman said. "This isn't the type of detail to withhold from a team leader. We need this explained better."

"I am not high enough in the List to demand every detail. However, it should be comforting to know I reviewed all the simulations many times. This will work. We'll get dropped long before the warheads go off."

"What is the purpose of the warheads?" Hoffman asked.

"They are a distraction, a screen for the screen. Some torpedoes fired from the Dotari ships carry armor. Some carry explosives. The ones with warheads will engage the Kesaht ships while the armor-bearing missiles deliver reinforcements to Syracuse. And we will hitch a ride on this one to the ambush point. The Kesaht bitches-of-sons will not know we're there. They will be busy exploding. No time to look for us," Gor'al said.

Hoffman drummed his gauntlet knuckles on his leg plate as he considered the plan and how to sell it to his team. "This can work. I don't like it, but I've been given worse plans to execute."

"Really?" Gor'al said in surprise.

"Really." Hoffman looked back at his team. Every one of them stared at him blankly.

****

Valdar scratched his beard as he looked over the Tactical Insertion Torpedoes' projected paths through the shattered moon. The time between a plan's inception and actual execution was always the hardest for him. Looking over missed details, internal doubts…demons arose to taunt his decisions. The temptation to squash the operation and find a more perfect solution to reinforce the defenders on Syracuse and beat the Kesaht fleet working through the moon was real…but tossing out the baby with the bathwater was not going to win this battle.

"Sir," Egan said from the other side of the holo tank, "Bat'ov hailing us."

"Dotari aren't known for second-guessing," Valdar said with a huff.

"Sir?" Egan's brows furrowed.

"Put him through."

The Dotari admiral appeared in a window at eye level with Valdar.

"Admiral, our engineers repairing the Crucible found a strange device transmitting through the network. Explain."

"The Kesaht held the gate for a—"

"It is a human device," Bat'ov said. "Your technicians refused to identify it. How are we to cooperate if we keep secrets from each other in the middle of a battle?"

"I don't know why my technicians would do such a thing," Valdar said, keeping his irritation in check. *The death of the Dotari Marine captain, now this.* "Can you…just show it to me?"

Bat'ov's image blinked off, replaced by a vid capture of a black box, the case cracked open, its internal electronics exposed.

"XO?" Valdar asked. "You were commo in a previous life."

125

Egan frowned and pulled the holo image over to him. As his fingertips danced over the box, scans from the techs aboard the Crucible populated around the device.

"Well?" Bat'ov asked.

"It's a routing hub," Egan said. "I recognize some of the components, but the rest is...the processor's fried. I don't know if that's from damage during the fighting or if it was caused by whoever tried to crack it open and peek inside. It's of human manufacture. That's for sure."

"Why is this a mystery to you?" asked the Dotari admiral, his quills bristling.

"The *Breitenfeld*'s been separated from High Command since we went into deep space to rescue the Golden Fleet." Valdar let the last words hang between him and Bat'ov, reminding the Dotari just what he'd done for their species. "The war with the Kesaht began while we were out of contact. It's entirely possible the Terran Union's placed new tech into the Crucibles under our control to trip up the Kesaht in the event they seized a Crucible. Send an emergency alert back to Earth. Foul up the graviton fields to prevent wormhole formation. Use your imagination."

The skin around Bat'ov's eyes flushed. "You are correct, Valdar. Please accept my apologies. This day is...trying."

"No apology needed," Valdar said. "I'll have my engineers pick the device apart soon as the Kesaht fleet are scrap and Syracuse invites us down for a victory celebration."

"Certainly...do you have any coffee beans? Asking for my staff."

126

"We have freeze-dried—"

Bat'ov spat and cut the channel.

"I may never understand them," Valdar said, looking to Egan. "What the hell is that thing, XO?"

"See this?" Egan pulled a component out of the device's holo and tossed it between the two officers. A flattened sphere with fiber optics poking from the edge like spokes spun slowly.

"I'm a ship driver, not a gearhead."

"Quantum flux generator, but not one like I've ever seen before," Egan said. "Too weak to affect wormhole formation—though it can send messages through the Crucible network."

"So Earth should know we're here," Valdar said.

"Techs said the Dotari detected it as the Crucible's self-repair went into overdrive after the fight to seize it from the Kesaht was over…but it's still too damaged for *us* to get word through," Egan said.

"The eggheads on Mercury made a leap in technology while we were in the deep void," Valdar said, shrugging.

"Something about this thing is…off," Egan said.

"There's a Kesaht fleet working through the moon coming to blow us out of space and we need a shoestring tackle to save the planet." Valdar grabbed the schematic and tossed it away. "Focus on the problem we have now. Mysteries can wait."

"Aye aye." Egan nodded quickly.

Chapter 9

Hoffman lowered into the small compartment behind the torpedo's warhead, went to a crash harness along the bulkhead and strapped himself inside. The rest of his team followed suit, grumbling about the setup. They'd done high-acceleration maneuvers before, but not in a vessel designed to explode against a target. Gor'al strapped himself in with confident, efficient movements, like the Dotari had done this a hundred times.

Hoffman resisted the urge to breathe a sigh of relief. His experience with Dotari technical advisors wasn't great, but Gor'al seemed enthusiastic and competent. It was a nice combination.

One by one his team took their places and were locked in. Strike Marine armor made it difficult for everyone except Opal to tighten the restraints without help. The doughboy contorted his arms at painful angles to get it done. As big as he was, he had been designed to maintain an impressive range of motion around each of his joints.

"Opal not fit good," Opal said. "Dotty-sized."

As their technical advisor, Gor'al insisted he have the "honor" of seeing to their safety. He stopped to look at Opal, checked everything twice, then shrugged.

"Your battle construct is bigger and smarter than I was led to believe," he said. "He's programmed not to harm me, I assume."

"Has he crushed your head yet?" Booker asked.

Everyone but Hoffman laughed. "Intelligence" wasn't a useful term when discussing the doughboy. He was neither dumb nor smart, just a bio-computer—or so Hoffman had been told repeatedly.

Duke was the last into the crash harness.

Gor'al made small talk in his thickly accented English. "I know all the unclassified accounts of Koen and Koensuu City. Your exploits as a marksman are very impressive."

Duke grunted acknowledgment.

Hoffman shifted in his seat, feeling an itch he couldn't reach. "They have unclassified parts of that battle already? The Dotari must do things differently than the Terran military."

"There are very few details. Some come from—how do you say—the noncommissioned officers butt-of-scuttle. Except mine is from the warrant-officer version of the same rumor network," Gor'al said. He was stepping back from Duke when something caught his attention. "You have food stuck in your lip?"

"It's a dip. Tobacco."

"What do you dip it in?"

"You don't dip it. It *is* dip," Duke said. "You want to try it?"

"What does it do?" Gor'al asked.

"It makes you a man." Duke reached into one of his cargo

pockets on his armor. "Here, I have a fresh can." He braced the round, flat can between his thumb and middle finger, then snapped it several times.

The Dotari's eyes widened. "Yes! I have seen many members of the human military do this. I must try some."

"Duke," King said, his voice hard and flat, "you know what that'll do to a Dotari?"

"What's the worst that could happen?" Booker asked, cueing other members of the team.

"He could puke in this very small space," Garrison said. "You see vents in here? Being covered in Dotty spew is possibly the only way this adventure can get worse."

Gor'al looked from face to face, seeking to understand the joke. His expression suggested he didn't quite get it but pretended he did. "I like this ritual of humor before glorious battle!"

Hoffman was looking up from his arm computer when he saw the Dotari Marine take a pinch of tobacco, lean his head back, and drop it into his throat.

"Booker, get ready to treat him," Hoffman said.

Duke's face turned bright red as Gor'al snatched another pinch and popped it into his mouth, chomping on the shredded tobacco leaves.

"What the hell are you doing?" Duke asked.

Gor'al pressed closer to the sniper. "This is delicious! Why have humans kept this secret from us?"

Duke closed the can and pulled it close to his body like a running back protecting a football with both hands. "Get back.

You can't eat it!"

"Just one more taste. Where can I find my own supply of this chewing tobacco?"

"I'm…fresh out," the sniper said.

Gor'al stood over Duke, opening and closing the cargo boxes on the sniper's armor. "I know you have more. Marines always have a secret stash of dip. This is known to me. I have watched the dippers dip and I must have just one…more…taste."

"Gor'al!" Hoffman shouted. "We have a mission to complete! Focus!"

Everyone but Duke howled with laughter. Hoffman felt himself smiling as he shouted down the Dotari technical advisor. "Just get buckled in, Gor. We can sign you up for the dip-of-the-month club back home or something."

"That would be a most excellent arrangement. Thank you, Lieutenant Hoffman. I look forward to cans and cans of chewing tobacco to celebrate our victory." He took a seat and waved for the Dotari engineers to approach. They swarmed around him, pulling straps, taking readings on handheld devices, and talking excitedly in Dotari.

"Well, our Dotty tagalong took to dipping better than I did," Booker said.

"I've created a monster," Duke said. "I heard they get high on coffee beans, now dip."

"Or you've created a market opportunity." Garrison tapped the side of his helmet. "We survive this, we might get rich selling your cancer gum to Dotties."

Gor'al suffered a second and third check of his harness, then waved the engineers away impatiently. "There. Now we are ready. Let's kick the tires and light the flames."

"Wait, who's our pilot?" Garrison asked.

Gor smiled. "Pilot? There is no pilot. All is automated. Our torpedo has a high-speed rendezvous with a Kesaht hull after it drops us off. Why sacrifice a pilot?" He shook his head, a motion that would have waggled his quills if not for the Dotari helmet.

"Why waste an entire Strike Marine team by strapping them onto a highly explosive warhead?" Duke asked.

Garrison shook his head as though denying an imminent disaster. "What if something goes wrong?"

Gor'al hissed and rustled his quills, a mannerism that caused his Dotari helmet to quiver very slightly. "Don't worry! We'll be smeared across the system before we even know something is wrong. Or atomized if the warhead explodes."

"That doesn't make me feel better."

Hoffman agreed with his breacher but didn't say anything.

Garrison looked to the team for support. "Anyone else feel better about that?"

"I find it oddly comforting," Max said.

"You would," Booker said.

"Doc's right. You're a freak, Max. Oddly comforting? Whatever," Garrison complained. "I don't want to be fired out of a cannon like a circus clown! I know explosives! Why would I want to be next to them while this piece of junk is bouncing toward wherever the hell we're going to get shot up this time?"

"You're right. This isn't safe. We should lodge a complaint," Booker said. "Anyone else vote to leave Garrison in daycare for this mission?"

"I second that," Max said.

"Stow it," King said. "Put on your mission faces."

"Yes! I know this movie," Gor'al said. "'Show me your war face.'"

Booker let off a middling war cry.

"Bovine leavings! You don't scare me," Gor'al said. "Work on it."

"He's not so bad," Max said. "Maybe we can keep him"

Garrison snorted. "He thinks we're going to live through this mission."

The hatch shut and vibrations from the crew bolting it to the hull rattled through the compartment.

"Stand by for launch in ten seconds," said a recorded Dotari voice in near-perfect English. "Ten, nine, eight…"

"Really?" Garrison asked. "Kind of abrupt. They didn't even offer us peanuts."

"…five, four, three…"

"Remember when you suggested shit-canning pilots in favor of automated Mule—" Booker started to say.

The launch pressed Hoffman into his harness with enough force that his vision grayed out. He nearly passed out, but the acceleration cut off quickly. Blood roared in his ears as his body normalized.

I need to check my tears, he thought as his eyes twitched and jerked. Disjointed images of his Marines calmed him. Opal stared back at him. The doughboy barely seemed to notice the gravity force caused by the acceleration.

Hoffman slowly regained his senses. The tactical display in his helmet was synchronized with the torpedo's navigation. Simple icons moved through a three-dimensional frame of grid lines. He was both impressed and disturbed by how fast they were moving away from the Dotari frigate.

No one spoke. The dark intensity of the situation brought them together as a team. In that moment, they were closer than brothers or sisters.

Hoffman keyed up a display on the inside of his visor.

The torpedo sped into the shattered sphere of the moon above Syracuse Prime as a vanguard of other munitions sprinted ahead. Hoffman tried to take in the enormity of what the display rendered. It was as though the moon had been expanded and could be put back together if anyone knew how the moving pieces fit.

He couldn't imagine navigating it successfully. Few human pilots had reflexes quick enough to avoid the densely situated space debris. Most of the larger asteroids maintained a consistent distance from one another, but smaller pieces were drifting in random arcs.

The Tactical Insertion Torpedo continued to weave through the debris at reckless speeds. He waited for the sound of impact and the end of their mission—and their lives.

Sensors went dead. Deceleration began, slowly at first, then like a spiraling bullet hitting water.

Hoffman flexed every muscle in his body, but it wasn't

enough to combat the rigors his body went through as they quickly slowed from their high rate of velocity. Stars bloomed in his vision and his world went dark. An instant later, the universe came crashing into his awareness once more.

"Stand by for deployment," said the recorded Dotari voice.

No one broke the ominous silence. They were still in the void, alone inside their helmets, as Hoffman mentally reviewed what should come next.

Warning lights flashed.

"Brace for deployment," the voice said. "Three, two, one, deploy."

Panels slid back, exposing the team to space until the only thing protecting his team was their void-rated armor. Hunks of the shattered moon hung in the distance. The chamber rotated and, swinging him around, Hoffman's crash harness released, propelling him from the torpedo. One by one, seconds apart, his team followed him. Last off was an anti-grav sled the size of a small car.

Hoffman swung his feet toward a hunk of rock the size of a football field, his visor marking it as their landing zone. He powered up his grav linings in his boots and cycled power into them. Breath fogged against his visor as his respiration increased. Dropping through void was different than moving through an atmosphere where the buttress of wind against his armor at least gave him a proper sensation of falling. Moving through space almost made it feel like he was watching the drop through VR.

Turning a foot to one side, he adjusted his course with a

short burst of anti-grav particles, eating up some of the battery life. He'd rather use a maneuver thruster, but stray gravitons weren't going to reveal his and his team's location. An unexplained heat source was easier to detect and would draw attention.

The hunk of moon looked like a broken mountain peak as he approached, but he knew that its negligible gravity wouldn't keep him attached. Void insertion onto an asteroid or hull was one of the more difficult missions a Strike Marine could carry out, but this was precisely what he and his team were trained for.

He glanced at his HUD to be sure the sled was on track. Losing it to the void would crimp the next phase. A small yellow dot showed the sled falling slightly ahead of his team.

"I have eyes on the sled," Garrison reported.

"I'm on your left," Max said to Garrison.

Hoffman watched their vectors converge. "Sound off," he ordered.

One by one, his team reported in. No one joked, bantered, or otherwise deviated from standard operating procedure. One mistake would kill them in the void. There was no Mule hovering nearby to rescue them if things went wrong.

"You're moving fast, L-T," King said.

"I want to be set up before the grav sled lands," Hoffman said. "The trick is not to land on it or let it land on us."

Seconds passed like minutes.

"How are we doing?" King asked, his voice strong but filled with void static.

"Five by five," Hoffman said, checking the dot icons in his

helmet display to be sure his team remained properly arrayed behind him. "We'll be on the asteroid momentarily."

Hoffman activated the grav linings in his boots and accelerated down. He hit hard, and his linings pushed him off the rock like a cork bobbing up from the water. He reversed the graviton flow and slammed to the ground, feet planted, then adjusted the pull from the linings and ran for a rock outcropping with loping strides.

The rest of his team landed at almost the same instant, forming a rough circle that would serve as their security bubble. The grav sled came down hard just outside their landing zone.

"Garrison, Max, secure the sled," Hoffman said.

"On it," said Garrison, taking the lead.

"Right behind you," Max said.

Hoffman's legs fought against the force from his grav linings as he landed

A denetrite warhead exploded with a flash overhead—part of Valdar's plan to confuse the Kesaht ships coming through the broken moon. A slight boom carried through the miniscule atmosphere of dust particles spread between the hunks.

"Team, report," Hoffman said as he scanned the surface of the asteroid through the sights of his gauss rifle. Haze filled the sky on this strange mini world.

"King."

"Booker."

"Duke."

"Opal, here, sir."

"Garrison and Max," Garrison said. "We're at the sled. Max can't get the diagnostic screen to turn on."

"Gor'al?" Hoffman turned around, counting heads.

"Yes, I am here," the Dotari said. "I am on the team? I'm honored."

Hoffman resisted the urge to lash out at the Dotari, another lesson learned working side by side with the aliens.

"We're moving to the sled's location and will set up a new security perimeter around it," Hoffman said.

Max staggered, then overcorrected, jumping several feet sideways on accident. "This place is freaky."

"Is that a technical term you commo guys use?" Booker asked, holding both hands out in front of her for balance.

Gor'al issued a staccato hiss that was probably meant to remain inside his helmet, but which broadcast through the external speakers. "The variable gravity takes getting used to, yes?"

"Fill us in, Gor," King said. "This information should have been in the briefing."

"The sentient species that lived on Syracuse destroyed this moon to thwart the Xaros invasion several thousand years ago. The Xaros set up graviton generators to prevent the debris from falling on the planet," Gor'al said.

"Wouldn't want to ruin their future colony world," Duke said dryly.

Gor'al clicked his beak several times. The sound boomed through their helmets. "I am reviewing the technical supplement. Who wrote this? Why don't human operational plans include annexes on the history of the writers? How else do I know if they're worth believing?"

"Drop it, Gor'al. Give me an update on the sled," Hoffman said.

An image from Max of the grav sled bumping up against a rock outcropping made Hoffman wince.

"Forward emitters damaged," Max said. "I can't fix it by the time we're supposed to be void-borne…maybe with a workshop and some good tools, but I'm a communications expert, not a mechanic. I can promise the EMP projector is working on the front of the sled, but might not be able to get the sled to actually move."

Gor'al bounded up high and over the rock where most of the team had taken cover. "I think I can help. Dotari know how to fix things."

"Great. Then get to it," Hoffman said. "And stop clicking your beak." He pulled his gauss rifle off his back and powered up the capacitor battery.

Several minutes passed as Hoffman stared toward the objective, wishing they were already there. "Progress report," he demanded.

King spoke on their private command link. "Gor'al is confident he can get it working. Not sure how long it will take him."

"Fine. Let's pull the camo cloak over the worksite. It'll slow us down, but we can't afford to get hit here."

Duke, Garrison, Booker, and Opal guarded the perimeter

with Hoffman and King checking each person's position from time to time as well as checking on Gor'al. Max set up his comm array but seemed to be struggling.

Hoffman squatted next to him. "What's the problem?"

"I can't get through. Too much interference. Too much dust out here. About what I expected," Max said.

Clouds of micro debris floated in a surreal mimicry of the Xaros-bound moon rocks, dissipating or coalescing from time to time. Watching the eternal dust dance turned Hoffman's guts.

"Do the best you can and let me know if you have any luck." Returning to the perimeter, he looked up and saw Kesaht ships working their way carefully through the shattered moon debris.

"We've got contact." Duke raised his new sniper rifle and looked through the optics, screen captures from which went out to the team. Kesaht clawships came into view. The destroyer-sized vessels had irregular-sized forward sections of the hull that reached out like bony fingers. Each digit served to focus energy into a beam that could rip through a ship's hull.

"Don't see the big boys yet," Duke said.

"Get a camo cloak over the sled and get concealed," Hoffman said. "There's enough ways this can go wrong. I don't want to eat a laser blast because some Rakka sailor was looking out a porthole at just the right moment."

He jumped over the rock and hurried toward the sled, where King and Max were already unfurling a tarp that changed colors as it moved.

Chapter 10

"Gor'al, you need to work faster," Hoffman said as he looked at the mission clock on his visor. By the operations order, the other Dotari Marine teams hidden throughout the broken moon were readying to launch on their targets.

"The forward graviton emitters sustained some damage," the alien said. "I just need to…reroute the auxiliary power and…" A burst of sparks came from the front of the sled and sprayed across Gor'al's helmet.

"Gluten-poisoned baked goods!" He fell back on his haunches, picked up a spanner from the ground and went back to work.

"You got one for us, sir?" King asked.

Hoffman zoomed in on a clawship flying around a rock fragment the size of a skyscraper.

"Mission calls for us to hit the closest one," Hoffman said, "keeps more than one team from going after the same target. But if we don't have a clear shot on the dreadnought, then we're just pissing in the wind."

"There is no movement of air to urinate in!" Gor'al whacked the side of the sled with his tool and the graviton generator came to life, sending a puff of dust out from the rock face.

"Thar she blows," Duke said, sending a live feed from his scope. A Kesaht dreadnought flew out from behind a distant moon shard. The hull looked like sections of bark removed from a tree and haphazardly nailed back to the trunk. Energy cannons dotted the hull in even lines, and a pyramid-shaped structure placed a third of the way up the ship from the engines served as the command and control center.

"Five miles from stem to stern," Duke said. "Not as big as the Toth monster that's crashed on Luna, but still…"

Garrison put a hand on a crate full of explosives on the grav sled. "I knew I should've packed more boom boom."

"Not the mission," Hoffman said. He switched to infrared and found a clawship a few dozen miles away. "There. That's the one."

A wavering in the void caught his attention, like air over a fire. He zoomed in and found a sphere, the surface swimming with fractals.

"That's the Xaros tech, right?" Max asked. "The gravity field generator?"

"One of a couple hundred through the moon," Hoffman said. "The mass from the Kesaht fleet must be upsetting the field keeping all the fragments in check…Load up."

"I'm driving!" Garrison hopped onto the sled and grabbed

the control stick. As the rest of the Marines got in, unpleasant memories of Strike Marine selection came back to him. Days in the surf around Coronado Island, harkening back to the American SEALs that later became the first Strike Marines, along with Green Berets and other special operation forces of the now-extinct Atlantic Union.

The sled spat out from under the camo tarp and pulled up and away from the moon fragment. Garrison steered them toward the Kesaht clawship Hoffman marked out as their target.

"Anyone having rigid inflatable boat flashbacks?" Max asked. "We may be in the middle of a broken moon, but at least we're not cold. And wet."

"We are now, as you humans say, up an estuary of feces without proper devices to propel us," Gor'al clicked his beak.

"You're giving me ideas for training when we get back to Earth," King said.

"Garrison, cut velocity," Hoffman said.

"Roger," the breacher said and the sled swayed beneath Hoffman's feet. He added, "We slow down, we're an easier target for that ship."

"We move too fast, we don't look like an asteroid pinging around," Hoffman said. "Offset your approach vector, not a direct course."

"So they don't maneuver away from us or shoot us," Garrison said. "That's way they pay you the big bucks, Lieutenant."

Additional ships moved through the debris sphere—

squadrons of crescent fighters, rows of clawships—all ahead of the dreadnought and the team's target ship. Enemy fighters and clawships fired on smaller asteroids along the dreadnought's path. The silent fireworks show spoke to just how easily their grav sled could be destroyed if it was detected.

"Whoever's in charge of their armada has some brass balls," Duke said. "Wonder how many ships they lost on the way through."

"Kesaht don't much care about casualties," Max said.

One of the larger ships opened fire on a rock nearly as large as the one Hoffman's team was crossing. At first, there were only a few energy beams, then the dreadnought opened up with everything it had. The asteroid came apart just as the ship touched it. Shields flared as it muscled its way through what should have been a fatal navigational error.

"Hold on," Garrison said and swerved the sled toward a clawship, coming up through its wake.

Hoffman's armor registered a heat warning as they passed through the outer edge of the ship's engine plume.

"I said I was glad we weren't cold," Max said, "not that I wanted to melt in my suit."

"Sensor dead zone." Garrison flipped the sled onto its side and slid along the ship's hull. The claws of the cannon emplacements seemed to be reaching for the *Breitenfeld* out beyond the sphere. "Did we get blown up? No. You're welcome," Garrison said as the sled grav-locked to the hull with a thunk.

"Max, get to work," Hoffman said as he swung over the

sled and locked his feet to the hull.

The communications tech removed a device shaped like a dinner plate and pressed it against the ship. Antennae sprouted from the plate, moving up and down.

"Jammer's in place," Max said. "They can transmit, but it won't get far. Multipath fading's our friend today."

"Got an entry." Garrison raised a hand and pointed to a slight depression in the hull.

"Breach bang clear," King said. "We're behind schedule."

"I swear they use pig iron for these hulls." Garrison placed small blocks of denethrite against heavy hinges, flipped away from the door and locked the bottom of his sabatons and one hand to the hull.

"Stand by for some atmo loss," the breacher said. "Then move for the inner air-lock breach. Fire in the hole. Three, two, one."

The hull quaked as the charges went off and the door went spinning into the void, propelled by a volcano blast of air. The gale of the ship's inner atmosphere continued for several seconds.

"What the hell?" Duke asked. "That whole ship's pressurized?"

"Was," Garrison said, glancing around the doorway. "No inner door?"

"Go go go!" Hoffman waved the breacher through.

Garrison pulled his gauss rifle off his back and swung into the Kesaht ship.

Hoffman followed behind Max as his team assaulted

145

through the breach point. The corridor leading into the ship was narrow, just wide enough for a single Strike Marine in armor. Hoffman almost pushed Max forward, as they were caught in a classic death funnel where a single shot could take out multiple Marines.

As flashes from Garrison's gauss rifle reflected off the inner walls, Max cut left around the corner and Hoffman went right. Rakka lay dead on the deck, most of which were bare-headed, their exposed flesh crusted with ice and almost purple from lack of oxygen.

Garrison rushed toward a Rakka leaning against a bulkhead, cracked the butt of his rifle against its head and shattered eye lenses. Air billowed out of the cracks and the Rakka fell to the deck, clutching at its face.

"Where's the bridge?" Hoffman asked.

"Hell if I know! Just killing right now, sir." Garrison shot a crewman as it came around a corner, splattering blood against the walls.

"Split up," Hoffman said, "two to a room. We need to own the bridge before they can recover."

Hoffman jumped up, using the pseudo muscles in his legs and a boost from his grav linings to carry him onto a catwalk. He ran toward a sealed set of double doors, the frame lined with pulsing red text.

"Brute force the door?" Max asked as he banged his fist against the bulkhead near the doorframe.

"Opal?" Hoffman half turned around and the doughboy

unsnapped the war hammer off his back.

Opal wielded the hammer with one hand, beating the head into the seam between the two halves. It knocked a deep dent into the metal. Opal tossed the hammer to Max and thrust his fingers into the small gap. Twisting to one side, Opal wrenched the door open like he was opening a can.

Hoffman tossed a flash-bang grenade through the opening and turned away. A blast of light cut through the opening and Hoffman charged inside Stunned and dying Rakka crawled across the deck.

On a raised command section of the bridge, a tall, lithe figure stood before wide windows looking out to the claws. The alien wore smooth, almost organic armor and clutched at its helmet. Hoffman shot stunned Rakka and rushed toward what he assumed was the ship's master.

Hoffman swung a punch into the alien's midriff, doubling it over, then threw it to the deck and put a boot against its neck.

"Clear!" Max shouted.

Opal kicked a downed Rakka hard enough to send it flying into a bulkhead with enough force to crack the alien's armor.

Hoffman looked over the controls and the alien text, all flowing script.

"Well done, team. Damn fine work," Hoffman said, glancing at the primitive knobs and slider bars on nearby workstations. Blocky lights flashed primary colors in patterns that meant nothing to Hoffman. "Gor'al, get control of this ship."

The Dotari pulled a line out of his gauntlet and fixed an

attachment to the end. He plugged it into a data port and screens appeared on his visor.

"The Ixio language is...different," Gor'al said.

"That's what this is?" Hoffman looked down at the lithe alien at his feet.

"The third race of the Kesaht collective," Gor'al said. "We rarely see them on the front lines. Likely because...well, look at it."

The Ixio beat weakly against Hoffman's leg and he lessened the pressure slightly.

"Ship's secure," King sent over the IR. *"All crew eliminated."*

"Good work, squat and hold until we can fire the cannons," Hoffman said.

Gor'al grabbed a control rod and twisted it to one side. The bridge lights dimmed. He clicked his beak and grabbed a handle on a round panel. Motes of light formed at the claw tips. He worked the controls and a holo of local space appeared near the forward windows. Their ship was on the outer edge of ships escorting the dreadnought.

"We have one hundred and eighty-four seconds before we're to open fire," Gor'al said. "The excrement is about to be broadcast."

"What? What's wrong?" Hoffman asked.

"Nothing." Gor'al placed his hands into a hologram cube and turned his fingers slightly, angling the ship toward the dreadnought. "Doesn't that mean things are fine?"

A white circle appeared in the holo field and a red dot pulsed outwards from the center.

"That is…unexpected," Gor'al said. "The firing controls are disabled. The system won't engage so long as the dreadnought is in the line of fire."

Hoffman grabbed the Ixio by the wrists and hauled it up. He brought the oversized eyepieces of the officer's helmet even with his own eyes then pushed his visor against the Ixio's head. A black eye the size of his palm wiggled beneath the alien's helm.

"You hear me?" Hoffman asked, letting vibrations carry his words over. "You can survive this. The Terran Union doesn't kill prisoners. You unlock the fire controls and you'll live."

"Murderer!" The Ixio thrashed like a fish on a hook, but Hoffman held it firm as the Ixio bent its head forward and pressed it to the lieutenant's visor. "Humans are a cancer. You've annihilated peaceful species. You will not do this to the Kesaht!"

"I don't know what you're talking about," Hoffman said. "You help us or we'll figure out our own way and then we'll leave you behind. Let you explain to your bug-eyed bosses just why this ship took a chunk out of the dreadnought. If anyone comes to rescue you, that is."

"Running out of time," Gor'al said.

"*Yuergada nisha,*" the Ixio said. "*Yeurgada nisha tol!*"

"Is that a ye—"

Air burst from the seams of the Ixio's armor and it went into convulsions. Hoffman tossed it aside and brought his rifle to bear. The alien shook violently for a few seconds, then went still. Violet blood seeped onto the deck.

"Oh, they have a suicide protocol," Gor'al said. "I'll put

149

that in my report."

"Shoot the damn cannons," Hoffman said, turning back to the controls and feeling useless in the face of the alien language.

"I cannot override the protocols from here," the Dotari said. "Likely a countermeasure against mutiny from the Rakka crew. Perhaps I could reroute the commands from the engines and fire it that way."

Hoffman glanced at the mission timer. "In the next twenty seconds?"

"Maybe no." Gor'al worked the controls and the ship veered away from the dreadnought. The white and red dots vanished. "But I suspect the rest of the Dotari Marine teams have encountered this same difficulty. The demon Murphy came on this mission."

"That dreadnought's going to figure out that something's off pretty quick," Hoffman said. "We need to be elsewhere when it turns its guns on us."

"I have an idea...one that might work," Gor'al said.

"Not the time for secrets," Hoffman said.

"I am going to blow up the Xaros graviton generator that holds these asteroids in position," Gor'al said with a quick nod of his head.

"Wait, that will—"

"Destabilize the moon and send the fragments around like a...a...hmm..." The Dotari touched his helm's chin.

"We'll be in a blender!" Hoffman felt a chill go down his spine.

The dreadnought opened fire, sending dozens of massive energy bolts out of the moon and toward the *Breitenfeld* and the Dotari ships.

"Our brothers are dying," Gor'al said. "Who are we to choose life?"

"Do it." Hoffman cursed himself as the Dotari went to work.

"Sir, can we get a sitrep?" King asked.

"Prepare to abandon ship," Hoffman sent. "We'll get one shot if we're lucky."

The Xaros graviton sphere appeared in the holo, and a pair of lines intersected over it. Energy built up on the claw tips and green lasers shot into a single point. A beam of energy slashed through the void, stinging Hoffman's eyes.

The sphere wobbled in the holo, a gash across the surface.

"That was less than satisfying." Gor'al cycled energy into another shot.

Beams flashed through space, all stabbing toward the Xaros sphere.

"Ah…" Gor'al snapped his fingers. "The other boarding teams came to the same conclusion. And who said Dotari Marines can't think on their talons?"

"Destroy that device before—" The deck bucked and sent Hoffman off-balance.

"Under fire!" Garrison shouted through the IR.

"Get to the sled," Hoffman sent and then grabbed Gor'al by the carry handle on his upper back and pulled him away from

151

the controls. He was dragging the Dotari to the exit when a sudden sick feeling formed in his stomach.

His feet slid across the deck, like he was being pushed by an unseen hand.

"I feel strange," Gor'al said. "Is it the chewing tobacco?"

The clawship lurched upward and sent the two crashing into the bulkhead.

"What the hell's going on out there?" Booker shouted over the IR.

"The graviton sphere—" Gor'al slipped from Hoffman's grasp and tumbled against the deck as the ship went end over end. "—It's destroyed. So the gravity...I'm going to be sick."

"Deck lock!" Hoffman put his feet flush to a bulkhead and activated his mag linings. The ship stopped spinning to his eyes, but his inner ear told a different story. "Get to the sled, Marines! We're leaving."

Reaching out, he caught Gor'al by the ankle and carried him off the bridge, locking one foot against the deck at a time.

Chapter 11

Sunrise on Syracuse Prime was as glorious as any Colonel Fallon had ever seen. The shadow of the fragmented moon hung near the horizon, a massive asteroid field held in stasis by ancient technology. In a way it was the most unique sky he'd ever witnessed.

Baer handed him an MRE.

Fallon stared at the food in wonder, accepting the plastic fork as he spoke. "You heated this up for me?"

"I figure you've eaten your share of cold slop, and you can't live on protein bars and anger forever."

"You're a good man, Baer. I should put you in for promotion."

"You keep saying that, but I have a more important ulterior motive."

"It's time for your situation report already, is that it?" Fallon said, shoveling the food in as he stood in the middle of shattered barriers. Glass and concrete dust covered everything in the city. Work crews couldn't rebuild the defenses fast enough, and ominous smoke was rising from Devastator's cooling vents.

"Yes, sir."

"Hit me with it."

"The rail gun overheated last night. Had to send Antony and his team out with rocket launchers to do what they could while Chief Connelly rebooted the cooling pumps," Baer said, watching Fallon shovel food into his mouth.

"Get to it, Baer. You're not the type to beat around the bush."

"Antony's team is MIA."

"MIA or KIA? Don't sugarcoat." Fallon finished the meal, pitched the trash, and sipped from his water tube.

"They're overdue and we've had no contact with them. If it was anyone but Antony and his group, I'd say definitely KIA. But they've been through some hard times. I won't believe they're dead until I see the bodies," Baer said. "We need them back here."

"They're on their own until we get some reinforcements from the fleet," Fallon said, knowing his lieutenant wouldn't like this. Other than Captain Quinn, Baer was his senior officer. He couldn't afford to have Baer rushing off on a search-and-rescue mission right now.

Baer tensed. "Sir, I—"

"Give me the numbers, the raw facts. We can talk as we walk. It's time for my review of the perimeter. The rail cannons are mission-critical. Antony knew that when he went out. That was why he went out."

"Yes, sir. Understood. I'd like to lead a mission to recover

Antony and his team."

"I'll take it under advisement. If—and that's a big if—I send someone after them, I will put you in charge of it. Good enough?"

"Yes, sir."

"I'm going forward."

"You won't have to walk far, sir. We're backed up as far as we can go. We're in a good position to inflict mass casualties on any force assaulting us, but we all know how indifferent their leadership is to spending lives. Rakka will attack anything and die screaming in your face."

"Put a kibosh on that talk whenever you hear it," Fallon said.

"Easier said than done, sir."

Fallon stopped and faced the Strike Marine officer with his hands on his hips. "You're a big man, an elite warrior of the Terran military. We need to be on the front lines showing these colonists how to fight. Show our metal and that'll put steel in the rest of them."

"Understood, sir." Grim-faced, Baer started walking. "Walk the line?"

"Let's go."

The inner defense was the strongest barrier they had: trenches excavated by civilian backhoes amidst the rubble of collapsed buildings, gun emplacements, and mine fields. Marines, militia, and civilians worked tirelessly to improve the depth and width of the trenches. Rakka warriors might be able to fight across it—swarming into it and murdering everyone they encountered—but their tanks couldn't drive over the deep barrier.

"That's one of our civilian work crews," Baer said, pointing to a group of women who looked like schoolteachers with shovels and sidearms.

"Warms my heart to see it," Fallon said. A heartbeat after he spoke the words, he saw the groups of dirty-faced children huddled nearby with fear in their eyes.

"There's no place else to put them. And you said bring the children if they could fire a weapon."

"Can they fire weapons?"

Baer held his palm horizontal and waggled it side to side. "Not so much. It'd be an accident waiting to happen and a waste of ammunition."

"Fix it. Get these noncombatants out of my defenses," Fallon said.

"I can't, sir."

"Then why are we here? Don't bring me problems with no solutions."

"Lenton and some of the other civilian leaders want to lead a breakout."

"That's stupid. Where would they go?"

Baer didn't answer because there was no answer.

"Is he ready to watch a bunch of civilians die?" Fallon asked. "Because escaping to...wherever...will be a bloody mess."

Baer spat tobacco on the ground in front of him. "That's what I told him. Made it real clear. Talked to him in private in case

I needed to rough him up or throw him in the brig. The thing is, I don't believe it's all his fault. These are civilians with families and no training for war. They're scared. They can't handle the wait between survival and the pants-shitting terror of the next attack."

Fallon lit a new cigar he had been saving for as long as possible. "So, what you're telling me is that the Kesaht are assaulting the planet with vastly superior numbers, my rail gun is overheating, my best Marines want to go gallivanting across the countryside on a buddy-rescue mission, and the civilians are getting ready to break and run—getting all these adorable children slaughtered in the process. Saint preserve us, you know how to ruin a man's day."

"Yes, sir."

"Thanks for the MRE, Baer."

"Everyone on the team spit in it for luck, sir."

"It was sealed."

"You think it was sealed, sir."

"You're a funny bastard. I ought to put you in for a promotion."

"Keep that in mind when I get to my next ask. Antony and I have served together for a long time. Blood brothers. We swore to—"

"Stupid," Fallon said. "Why the hell would you make promises you can't keep? You know better than that, Baer. War isn't the place for hope and plans."

Baer didn't respond.

"We never leave anyone behind unless there's no other

choice. Taking oaths and making promises is both unnecessary and detrimental to accomplishing whatever mission you're assigned to. I've left people behind, Baer, a lot of people—but only because there was no other choice. You want to lead a team outside the wire and find him?" Fallon asked.

"Yes, sir."

"Denied. Antony's team is my responsibility. I'll lead a scout mission to rescue them. You're coming with me." The colonel pointed to a captain in the trench line with a field dressing over his thigh. "You're lucky Franks is wounded, yet competent. If we didn't have him to hold down the fort, you'd be cooling your heels back here eating pouch mush and drinking shit coffee. Let's go 'hey you' a team."

Chapter 12

Hoffman was the last out of the clawship. Space spun around them as the ship continued its free fall through the disrupted gravity field. He stomped toward the sled where his team was already embarked, swaying from side to side with the motion of the hull.

"Worst. Roller coaster. Ever." Garrison powered up the sled from the driver's seat.

When a shadow passed over Hoffman, he looked up and saw distant moon fragments moving like driftwood on a slow river. The clawship completed its rotation and a massive asteroid came into view, growing larger by the second.

"Pretty sure that's coming right for us!" Duke shouted.

Hoffman took a longer stride and the hull moved just out of the grasp of his mag linings. He floated off the ship with a string of expletives.

"Hang on!" Garrison released the sled and it lifted away. He sent it speeding forward, then it seemed to stop midflight, yards away from Hoffman.

"What're you waiting for?" King pointed to the lieutenant.

"Gravity's all funky." Garrison shimmied the sled from side to side, but it stayed the same distance from Hoffman. "It's like trying to steer through waves."

The oncoming asteroid grew closer, and Hoffman wondered just how hard it would hit.

"Get clear!" Hoffman waved and went back, head over heels, with a sudden pull from behind. He felt like a pea rattling in a can as gravity went insane. The sled, the clawship and the oncoming rock flashed across his visor.

Something grabbed his ankle and his armor nearly tore as a sudden acceleration flung his arms up.

Opal slammed Hoffman to the deck of the sled and lay his massive bulk over the lieutenant, pinning him down as the sled swerved through the void and then righted itself, bringing the madness to an end.

"Sir OK?" Opal asked.

"I'm good, big guy. Thanks for the save." Hoffman patted the doughboy on the shoulder and sat up, looking over the edge of the sled. He slammed himself flat.

The rogue asteroid hurtled overhead amid shouted warnings from the Marines. Hoffman got to his feet and watched, wide-eyed as the rock pulverized the clawship into a million pieces. Stray bolts of energy crackled through the debris as the energy cannons dissipated.

"And you're welcome!" Garrison shook a finger in the air. "Thank you all for flying Garrison Void Transport. Do note the lack of bathroom facilities in the event you need to change out your pants."

"I hate you, Garrison," Booker said. "But I'm alive so I don't hate you that much."

"The Xaros graviton emitter seems to have stabilized." Gor'al flipped a screen up from his gauntlet and tapped with one hand. An image of a sphere with shrinking gauges came up on Hoffman's visor "It seems this Xaros technology possesses the same self-repair capability as the Crucibles. I'll note this in my report."

"Heads on a swivel," Hoffman said. "Still plenty of rocks moving around."

"Return to the *Ereit* or stay put?" Garrison asked.

"Eyes open. Mouth shut," King said. "You want to waste power fighting through surf and dodge multi-ton projectiles or wait until things simmer down?"

Light flashed from port and Hoffman leaned over sled's low sides. The Kesaht dreadnought was firing on a moon fragment that looked like black ice, hundreds of yards long and closing on the ship. Blasts knocked off massive chunks, spraying the void with glittering crystals.

"Come on," Duke said. "Let's catch a break here."

The dreadnought's cannons fired faster and several burst apart from the strain. The obsidian-like fragment broke in half, sending one part up and away from the ship. The other pierced the shields, leaving a tear as it slashed down the hull like a scythe. Atmosphere burst out of the tear and fire flared briefly before succumbing to the void.

The fragment came to a stop in the hull, sticking out like the hilt of a dagger stabbed into flesh. Lights flickered over the dreadnought's hull and the ship listed to one side. Fire and heat from the engines died away.

"Ha! That got him!" Max beat a fist against the sled.

"I doubt this," Gor'al said. "Kesaht capital ships are of a modular design."

"Get to the point," Hoffman said.

"The damage is localized to the starboard side. The ship could still fire and maneuver once they contain any secondary effects like power surges, atmosphere loss and—"

"It's not out of the fight completely," Hoffman said.

"Yes, as I was saying, it—"

Hoffman put a heavy hand on the Dotari's shoulder and Gor'al stopped talking.

"But it's vulnerable," King said. "Max, why hasn't the *Breitenfeld* or the Dotties finished it off yet?"

An antenna lifted out of Max's armor and unfurled into a dish. The dish bent back toward the outer edge of the shattered moon and wiggled from side to side, and a comms channel to the ship popped up on Hoffman's visor. He opened it with the flick of a finger over his gauntlet.

Admiral Valdar appeared, emergency repair tape over the front of his void suit and a spider crack on one side of his helmet.

"Hammer Six reporting in," Hoffman said. "Enemy ship disabled but not destroyed. Mission didn't go as planned."

Valdar glanced up, an eyebrow raised. "Hammer, my ship's taken a beating. We're dead in space and I sent the Dotari fleet through the moon to break the siege," Valdar said. "Can you make extraction? The Dotari spared a corvette to pick up you and their Marines."

A waypoint appeared in the broken moon, clear on the other side of the space disrupted by the damaged graviton device.

"No way, Lieutenant," Garrison said, flicking a finger against the control panel. "We're almost black on power as it is. Can't coast there after accelerating. We could make the *Breit*...probably."

"Admiral, the enemy ship is off-line, but my tech advisor says it's not completely out of the fight," Hoffman said.

"Concur," Valdar said, shaking his head slowly. "It's going to be a race. Whichever ship gets their main guns online first will destroy the other. If I was a betting man, I wouldn't put money on my ship."

Hoffman swallowed hard, then looked to the listing dreadnought. "We'll buy you time, sir."

"The Dotari can handle the Kesaht in orbit," Valdar said. "No need to risk yourselves. We've almost got the battle won. I want you and your Marines to—"

Hoffman reached over to Max and twisted the IR dish to one side, breaking the channel.

"It's the *Breitenfeld*," Hoffman said. "Ship of miracles. She won the Ember War," he said and looked at Gor'al, "and saved the Dotari more than once. We are not going to sit around and watch

163

those Kesaht bastards destroy her."

"Oorah, Lieutenant," King said.

Duke rapped the butt of his sniper rifle against the sled. Max and Booker hit their fists over their hearts twice, a salute to Saint Kallen. Garrison wiggled into his seat and flashed a thumbs-up.

Gor'al looked around at the human Marines. "So…we're going to assault the dreadnought? By ourselves?" the Dotari asked.

"Don't worry," Garrison said, shrugging. "We have a doughboy."

"Opal fight." The battle construct gave an exaggerated nod.

"Well," Gor'al said as he tapped against his gauntlet computer, "the dreadnought's bridge is still intact. Perhaps a pinpoint assault on the ship master would disrupt the ship long enough to—"

"Exactly what I was thinking," Hoffman said. "Punch it, Garrison!"

The sled accelerated and dove toward the dreadnought.

Chapter 13

The *Breitenfeld* lurched to port and Valdar's feet slid against the deck. He clung to the holo table as the ship listed nearly to its side.

"XO, what the hell is wrong with gravity?" Valdar asked as a slew of new damage reports came up in the holo tank. He ignored the minor damage from the event that just gripped his ship and returned his focus to the squadron of Kesaht clawships and a few cruisers that had come through the shattered moon.

Crescent fighters swirled around the strike carrier in a dogfight against Dotari and a few Terran Union Eagles. Kesaht fighters exploded in small sunbursts as the allied ships recovered faster from whatever had just happened.

"Firing solution ready," Utrecht called out.

"Hold fire," Egan said and held up a hand. "There's some sort of graviton disturbance and it could—"

"Send it!" Valdar ordered.

The ship bucked as the rail cannons shot hypervelocity rounds toward the emerging ships. The munition sliced through the engines of a Kesaht cruiser, splitting it into spinning parts that joined a wave of asteroids let loose from the moon.

"Where's the dreadnought?" Valdar moved the holo tank to inside the moon. Fragmented images of the massive enemy ship, its hull ripped open by a jagged rock fragment nearly the size of the *Breitenfeld*, drifted inside the moon.

"Admiral Valdar," said Bat'ov, appearing in the holo, "the disturbance within the moon appears to be localized."

The image shifted to the entire sphere. A lower section of asteroids pinched and pulsed in chaos but the rest of the moon was almost serene by comparison.

"Incoming!" Egan shouted. Ruby dots appeared in the void and grew brighter as the clawships' energy beams readied. Coherent energy spat out and struck the *Breitenfeld*'s flank. Scorch marks drew black lines as wide as a fighter down the hull, sending vibrations through the whole ship.

An explosion rumbled through the ship and the panels on Valdar's holo table snapped off. Lights in the ceiling went red as main power failed.

"We just lost battery stack three," Egan said, touching the side of his helmet.

A schematic of the *Breitenfeld* appeared on the inside of Valdar's visor. Crimson damage reports flooded in from the rear third of the ship—damage to the hull looked like a giant beast had swiped claws across her.

"Engineering," Valdar said, opening a channel. His chief engineer didn't answer, and a casualty report appeared a moment

166

later. Dead.

"Move damage-control teams to the generators," Valdar said. "We're dead in space, just waiting for the Kesaht to—"

A clawship beam shot past the bridge. A blinding wave of ruby light washed over the workstations and more than one crewman cried out.

"I prefer it when they miss," Egan said.

"Valdar!" Bat'ov shouted through an emergency radio frequency. *"Are you alive?"*

"My ship's off-line but we can get back in the fight," Valdar said.

"The clawships overloaded when they fired on you. All are destroyed," Bat'ov said. *"The final cruiser will not be a problem in..."* An explosion blossomed far ahead of the *Breitenfeld. "No longer a problem. I suggest we—"*

"Take your ships and get to Syracuse," Valdar said. "Set an alternate course through the stable sections of the moon—it will screen your approach. Then you must take out the Kesaht ships in low orbit. Plan remains the same. My ship will catch up to you."

"The dreadnought is still a threat," Bat'ov said. *"It's suicide for me to launch an attack on it now, but I can leave a squadron of destroyers behind to protect you and strike when the opportunity presents itself."*

"Negative. You need every gun to break the siege. Get moving, Bat'ov."

"What about you?"

"Our damage...we can handle it. We don't have a knife in our belly like the dreadnought. We'll recover before them. I'll bet

167

my life on it."

"And the Keystone? The Council of Firsts insisted I preserve that device."

"The Council of Firsts isn't here. Are you going to get your ass in gear or do I have to get angry?"

There was a brief pause and Valdar heard several Dotari squawking at each other.

"Our ass gear has laid in a new course. Good luck, Admiral."

"*Breitenfeld*, out." Valdar banged a fist against the dead screens of his holo tank. "XO, you have the bridge. I'm going to engineering to see the damage for myself."

Chapter 14

Garrison cut power to the sled's engines as it closed on the dreadnought. The massive shipped rolled over slowly, trails of air seeping out of cracks in the hull. Gas traced along the obsidian shard, condensing into an icy sheen.

Max pointed to the pyramid-shaped command structure. "This assault going to be personal, sir?" he asked.

"We don't need to shoot them in the face," Hoffman said. "We'll latch onto the pyramid and blow it with denethrite. You've got more, Garrison?"

"Plenty," the breacher said, "loads more party favors in the case Gor'al's sitting on."

The Dotari tensed up, then looked down between his legs.

"Little denethrite goes a long way," Garrison said. "But for a case like this, I'm all for being generous. Void charges are forgiving, no atmo to carry a blast wave."

"Got bogies," Duke said. "Looks like an outer-cordon combat air patrol." Icons for crescent fighters several kilometers off the prow of the ship came up on the Marines' visors.

"Don't wave to 'em," Garrison said.

"Should we prepare the explosives?" Gor'al asked. "There are a number of windows on the command structure and I doubt the Kesaht will ignore us."

"Just tell them you're there to wash the windows," Booker said.

"I don't think that will work." Gor'al shook his head quickly.

"On approach," Garrison said and tightened his grip on the controls.

"Get us near the base of the pyramid," Hoffman said. "We blow the spars, we could pop the command center like a cork."

"Somebody film that," Garrison said, giggling.

The sled dipped and inverted, matching the angle of the dreadnought's dorsal hull, lights blinking across the surface amid a low fog of leaking air. Tendrils of flame wavered along cracks in the armor.

"Half the ship's in bad shape," Booker said.

"This is one time I'm fine with kicking them while they're down." Duke pulled the stock of his sniper rifle against his shoulder.

"About to set down," Garrison said. "This is a pop-and-drop so I need—"

His control panel exploded as a burst of energy bolts snapped past the prow.

"Bogies!" King shouted.

The sled sped along the dreadnought's hull. Hoffman

looked up as ship passed overhead.

"Garrison?" Hoffman said, grabbing Gor'al and yanking him off the case of explosives.

"Lost all controls. Bail out!" Garrison tossed a broken steering column away.

Opal's heavy gauss cannon snapped as the doughboy opened fire from the rear of the sled, the recoil sending the craft into a wobble. Kesaht crescent fighters jinked from side to side as they closed on the Marines.

"Bail!" Hoffman grabbed Gor'al under the front of his breastplate and threw the Dotari up toward the ship. He got the explosives case by a handle and turned as the rest of the team jumped up and away—everyone but Opal.

Hoffman reached for the doughboy as an energy bolt ripped down the side of the sled. Hoffman went flying, the case still in his grip.

"Opal!" Hoffman struggled to right himself as the mass of the case threw off his balance. He hit the ship and the case dragged him against the armor plating until the case whacked against a raised section of armor and Hoffman came to a stop. He winced, fearing the shock-sensitive explosives were about to go off.

When his world didn't end in a bright white flash, he rolled over and saw the sled flying away from the dreadnought. Opal's heavy gauss cannon flashed.

"Opal, can you hear me?" Hoffman asked through the IR. "You need to bail out. Bail out, doughboy, that's an order!"

Crescent fighters cut through the void overhead, cannons

171

blazing.

The sled exploded.

"Opal!" Hoffman let the case go and took an uneasy step. He checked his IR connections. The doughboy was off-line.

"No...no..." Hoffman detached his gauss rifle from his back and aimed it at a fighter as it blew through the debris field.

A hand slapped the barrel down and King grabbed the lieutenant by the shoulder and turned him around.

"He's gone!" King said, holding Hoffman's arm.

"He can't be. I promised him I'd—"

King slapped the side of Hoffman's helmet. "Sir, you need to get back in this fight. Now."

Pain welled up in Hoffman's chest, but he choked it down, took a deep breath, and pushed Opal out of his mind. Glancing around, he picked up the explosives. They'd landed far from the command structure, almost a mile away. Air seeped from cracks in the hull like they were atop a field of cooling lava.

"Head count," Hoffman said. "Need a head count."

"Down one," King said sternly. "How do we continue this mission?"

"We need...we need to make an EVA movement to the pyramid," Hoffman said. "Double echelon front. Speed is our armor right now."

Duke's voice broke through the radio chatter. *"We've got trouble. One hundred meters from our location, there's a bay door sliding open. Looks like Rakka and Sanheel in void suits. I guess the grunts are smart enough to function in space."*

The Rakka grunts stomped forward as Hoffman and King took cover against a broken section of the hull. Hoffman lifted his rifle optics over their cover and watched through a screen on his visor as the Kesaht foot soldiers made their way across the hull. From their oversized metal boots to massive shoulder pauldrons and skull-shaped helmets, they looked like nightmares from a forgotten age.

The Sanheel were enormous centaurs, but they moved with more grace in the micro gravity. Their armor was just as exaggerated as the Rakka's but more refined. Banners streamed from short poles on the back of their armor, twisting in random directions with no atmosphere or gravity to influence them. Like the Rakka they led, the Sanheel officers moved in lockstep precision until close enough to charge.

The Rakka pounded gauntleted fists against chest plates, a menacing effect even without sound.

When the largest, most flamboyantly attired Sanheel raised a hand over his head, the quick-stepping march became a full charge.

"So much for not getting noticed," Max said.

Hoffman looked back across the damaged hull. The attackers had come from the undamaged half of the ship. He glanced over the edge of their cover and a slug bounced off the edge, just missing his face.

"Garrison, there should be an entrance fifty meters to our five o'clock," Hoffman said. "Take Gor'al and make us a door. King, lay down suppressive fire and cover their move."

"But wouldn't it be better to have more guns in the...discussion later." Gor'al followed Garrison in a low crouch as they hurried away.

"Take 'em out." Hoffman came up from behind cover and opened fire. Gauss bullets smacked into Rakka, sending them floating away off the hull in a spray of blood. A round hit Hoffman in the shoulder, fouling his aim for a moment, but he stayed up and kept shooting.

Precision shots from Marines blunted the Kesaht attack. Rakka died in droves, but the Sanheel prodded their soldiers forward. Hoffman switched his rifle to high power for the last gauss shell in his magazine and fired. The recoil sent him sliding a few inches back. The bullet tore an arm off a Sanheel and the alien went down, clutching at the blood and air spewing from the hole.

Hoffman ducked back down and slapped in a new battery and magazine.

"Sir, you're right about that door," Garrison sent over IR. *"Bit of a mess to open though."*

"The longer you take, the worse it gets out here." King ducked next to Hoffman.

"You'll know when I've got it open," the breacher said. *"No time for subtlety. No, Gor'al, the blue one goes on top."*

Hoffman popped up and watched as the Sanheel moved toward a rent in the hull.

"Not like them to break off," Hoffman said as a realization hit him. He looked down the hull and saw three crescent fighters coming in low.

"Bogies!" Hoffman ducked against cover as a flash of light cast shadows against the hull.

Duke was on his feet, his sniper rifle lifting back from the recoil of a shot, but he brought the rail gun down and fired again. A crescent fighter exploded and the other two opened fire.

Duke held his ground as energy bolts stitched across the deck. He fired again, the recoil slapping his back against the hull. Duke released his mag locks and went sliding.

A second fighter nearly vaporized as a hyper-velocity slug tore it to pieces. The last fighter jinked from side to side, evading the debris.

The fighter snapped overhead and Duke spun around, still on his back, to bring his rifle to bear. He fired again and the last fighter split in half. The recoil sent him sliding back to the Marines hunkered down against cover.

Locking his boots, Duke tossed an empty magazine away as he came up to a crouch.

"Show off," Max muttered.

"You missed your first shot," Booker said, firing over the hull plating.

"I want crap from you, I'll squeeze your head." Duke stood and drilled a round through the broken armor the Sanheel used for cover. The upper torso of an alien officer shot up, severed from the rest of its body.

When the ship rumbled, Hoffman looked back to where he'd sent Garrison and the Dotari. The breacher swung around a raised part of the hull and waved them over.

"Move, move!" King fired as he backpedaled toward the opening.

Hoffman emptied a magazine toward the Kesaht as he crossed the distance, ignoring the haphazard return fire from the remaining Sanheel.

A hatch was partially blown off its hinges, revealing an inner air-lock door. Garrison pulled out a crowbar and cracked the inner door open. He pulled it open and Max was the first one through, rifle up and ready.

Hoffman went through, then froze. He'd left the explosives case behind. When he turned around, he saw Booker had it and his face flushed with embarrassment.

Garrison slammed the air-lock door as King came through last.

"Check suit integrity," said the gunnery sergeant. "Air and round count now. Someone double-check Duke's air."

"One time," the sniper grumbled, still sore over nearly suffocating during the mission to the Dotari Golden Fleet.

Hoffman went to a corner and quickly peeked down the passageway where low red emergency lighting blinked on and off and tendrils of smoke clung to the ceiling.

"Micro atmosphere," Booker said. "Don't spill your air, Marines."

"Ammo cross leveled," King said. "All suits green for power. Amber for oxygen."

"Where…we've got to figure out where we are in the ship," Hoffman said. As he looked back to the air lock, memories of Opal flooded over him: The first day his doughboy platoon imprinted on him during the Ember War. Opal beside him when the first of his kind went dark, shutting down from system degradation. All the time in training when Opal never left his side.

Sorrow gripped his heart, but he kept his composure. He couldn't take the time to grieve. He had a team to lead.

"This data port is off-line." Gor'al removed a wire from a plug near the air-lock controls. "I suggest we use the under passageways."

"If you can't access the ship," Max said, "how do you know about 'under passageways'?"

The Dotari pointed at Max's feet. Beneath the grated metal deck was an unlit hallway, with a frozen slurry of brown material running along a groove in the bottom.

"Oh," Max said.

Hoffman looked around the upper passage, its dimensions large enough for three Sanheel at a time.

"That must be for the Rakka," King said, stomping a foot on the grate to indicate the hallway beneath their feet.

"Leave it to the Dotari to spot the caste system," Gor'al said. "I suggest we take the low road. Less chance to encounter the big ones."

Hoffman snapped his Ka-Bar out of his forearm housing and slashed through where deck plating joined together. Lifting a grate, he waved his team through.

"What's next, sir?" King asked on a private channel.

"Keep moving. Get to the command center and blow it to

hell—or find some other way to keep this ship off-line." Hoffman dropped down into the Rakka hallway and let the grate shut.

King stepped close to him and said, "I'm sorry." Hoffman nodded but didn't say anything. "Opal was a good Marine," King added.

"He was. Better than I'll ever be." Hoffman shook off despair and followed his team.

Chapter 15

Fallon stopped, looked, and listened. Darkness pressed on his senses when it should have reassured him. Strike Marines owned the night...until they didn't.

The Kesaht artillery park glowed on the other side of a ridge. He wondered what the hell they were doing to have such careless light discipline. Kesaht forces chanted rhythmically, then cheered. Scattered gunshots echoed through the night and then a flare went up over the enemy position.

Fallon and his team froze. The shouting continued as the dirty-yellow flare drifted downward and died.

"What are they doing?" Baer asked, invisible in the fresh darkness.

"That wasn't directed at us. Advance. We're on the clock." As he moved, Fallon scanned the immediate area with night-vision optics and forward-looking infrared sensors. Technology made the horizon blaze like a green sun. "No patrols in the sector."

Baer materialized out of the shadows as he cleared his zone. The big man moved like a hunting cat on two legs. "Probably because this terrain is tore up like the devil's guts. I still don't like it. How can they not have patrols this close to their artillery? When it looks too good to be true, it is too good to be true."

"If they're getting piss-face drunk and shooting fireworks, great. Unfortunately, I've got a good idea what they're celebrating." Fallon swept his weapon right and left, scanning his zone every few steps. "We're not as close as I thought. There's at least one more escarpment between us and the artillery. The Kesaht are idiots, but not complete idiots. They have the high ground. It'll take some work to find a good observation post."

The chorus of Rakka chants and booming drums echoed through the night, the volume growing until the clamor exploded in a finale of shouts and boot stomping.

Fallon pointed at an escarpment shaped like an anvil. "Let's get up there and see what we see. Should be high enough to look down on them."

"Yes, sir." Baer signaled Crimson and Gold squads toward their new objective.

Fallon stalked through the shadows, tracking Baer and the other Marines on his HUD. The small dots reassured him. They were green across the board and ready for action.

Scraggly underbrush and narrow trees like aspens stained gray provided concealment for the next hundred meters. They arrived at an open area split by a creek.

"Crimson squad, cross and set up security. Gold Squad has overwatch," Baer said.

Fallon waited, then moved at the center of Gold Squad.

Once the entire team was across, they made good time toward the sliver of high ground above the Rakka artillery park.

More drum beating, shouting, and small-arms fire punctuated the noise in the camp.

"Crimson for Gold, we have eyes on a pack of Rakka foot soldiers. They act alert, but I think they're pretending. It will take a while to go around them."

Fallon took several steps to find a good position before answering. "Define 'pack.' Platoon or squad-sized element?"

"A diminished squad, looks like five or six. I can't see them all at once so I'm not sure," the Crimson Squad leader answered. "They're equipped like a security patrol. Only thing missing is their motivation."

"Gold is in position to support. Silenced sidearms and knives. No need to alert other patrols if there are any," Fallon said. "Can't have them skulking about when we come back this way."

He marked his target with an infrared designator while his team selected other targets. They proceeded slowly, pausing to see if their victims had detected their approach.

Fallon came within arm's reach of his victim.

"On my mark," Fallon whispered within his helmet as he silently eased the well-machined bayonet from his right gauntlet. His sealed helmet contained the sound of his voice as he took another short step. "Three, two, one, mark."

He thrust the blade into the base of the Rakka warrior's neck, neatly slicing through crude armor. Grabbing his victim, he lowered his dying enemy to the ground.

"Report," he said.

One by one, his team checked in.

"Good work." Fallon continued up an animal trail and saw the Kesaht base for the first time.

Rakka barracks were clustered into three large, random groups. Near the center was an ammo depot, easy to identify by pallets of ordnance that begged for an airstrike or sabotage. Armored vehicles and trucks were strung around the perimeter in a formation that was almost adequate for defense of the base.

"I don't see their main battle tanks," Fallon said.

"They could be hunting the Dotari Armor."

Fallon grunted. "Whoever organized their camp should be shot. If I had a full battalion right now, we could take this artillery park," Fallon said.

"If wishes were fishes, sir," Baer said.

A troop of Sanheel officers burst from a flamboyantly huge tent, shouting a bawdy song and waving swords and pistols in the air.

"That's something you don't see every day," Baer said, shifting his position and making notes on his arm computer.

Elsewhere in the camp, Sanheel brutalized a squad of Rakka for no apparent reason—yelling at them and cracking whips over their heads.

"No discipline. No attempt to clear away underbrush or trees within the camp. Their officers are worse than their men." Fallon surveyed the scene. "There's the commotion that we've heard for the last hour."

Lashed to the side of a tracked transport were several Marines: Antony and several others. One's head drooped low and blood covered his armor, pooling below his hanging feet. A trio of Rakka warriors took turns throwing knives at them, the crude blades bouncing off the Marine's armor. There wasn't a Sanheel officer near the carnival of violence to put them in check. Antony and the Marine next to him flinched each time a blade struck, but others didn't move.

"Permission to let loose our sniper, sir," Baer growled.

"Negative."

"Sir! There's at least one dead Marine down there and two more will join him if we don't do something," Baer said.

"We snipe now, what will happen to the prisoners?" Fallon said. "Take three men and prepare to infiltrate. I'm not using our sniper or the tridents until we get those men clear. Trust me, Baer, the men down there wouldn't thank me if I unleashed hell while they're still tied up. We're waiting on a chance to not blow up Antony and his men. Comms, get the Dotari Armor on the horn now." Fallon waited seconds that felt like minutes, keeping a close eye on his lieutenant "We need a distraction. Don't rush to failure, Baer. You're better than that."

"Yes, sir," Baer growled.

The communication specialist, a young lance corporal who appeared even younger each time he tried to grow his peach-fuzz beard, looked up nervously. "I have a connection but it's weak. Patching you through, Colonel."

Fallon nodded brusquely as he turned away to hail the

Dotari Armor. "Gold 6 for Dotari Armor."

"Talon for Gold, your signal is poor," said a heavily accented Dotari voice.

"You're coming in well enough," Fallon said and provided his coordinates. "What is your position relative mine?"

"Close. Will there be a fight?"

"Yes. We need a diversion. Can you draw them from their camp?" Fallon asked as he studied the camp and the terrain around it. The disarray of the Rakka infantry didn't change the number of Rakka and Sanheel who would charge down the hill when provoked. The artillery crews and rocket teams were not part of the drunken shit show. Fallon saw them guarding their beloved guns like living gargoyles.

He suspected there was at least one company of tanks in the area and feared another wave of Kesaht forces would soon slip past his rail gun.

"We have eyes on the Kesaht base. Soon they will feel our wrath," the Dotari leader said.

"What's your name, Talon 1?" Fallon asked.

"I am Fal'tir. I am Armor."

"This will be a dangerous mission, even for your lance," Fallon said.

"Of course. If it was easy, anyone could do it," the Dotari lance leader said. "We are on the way.

"It has to be now. Five minutes ago would have been better."

"We shall strike in one minute. We will begin with a

ranged attack, then show ourselves and entice them to pursue us," Fal'tir said.

****

"Baer, what's your status?" Fallon asked, feeling the silence of the night like a lead weight.

Even with his helmet on, Baer spoke softly. "Very close to the Kesaht perimeter. Looks like they're taking a break. Maybe they all passed out. Hold on, Colonel. I've got to take care of something."

"Don't get cocky, Baer." Fallon watched, suppressing his innate need to verbally kick the Strike Marine's ass.

Baer crept behind two Rakka slouching on rifles. With a knife already extended from the sleeve of his armor, he drew a second blade from his harness.

"Risky," Fallon muttered with his mic turned off.

Baer stabbed both sentries under the base of their skulls. Two of his Marines stepped forward to catch the falling bodies.

"I don't hear the commotion from our targets. Are they done throwing knives at my friends?" Baer asked.

"They're busy sharpening said knives." Fallon left out other details, not wanting to send the lieutenant and his rescue team into a blind rage. The Rakka not sharpening their throwing knives were stabbing dead Marines with bayonets and shovels. He flinched each time a blade hit a body. A vein in his forehead throbbed so hard he thought the Marines around him must see it

185

through his visor. *I'm going to kill every last one of you sons of bitches.*

"Copy. Waiting on the signal to recover our people," Baer said.

Fallon spotted a rustle in the tree branches less than a kilometer from the camp. "I have eyes on the Dotari. They're about to make some noise. Stand by, Crimson. Gold 6 for Talon, be advised you are approaching unfavorable ter—"

"Moving to the truck park." Baer's harsh whisper interrupted him. "Good concealment and no guards seen. Too easy to pass up."

"Crimson, hold position. Sanheel on patrol." Fallon toggled channels. "Gold for Talon, do you copy?"

"Fal'tir does copy but does not see what there is to be done to correct the situation. We are armor."

Fallon muted his microphone, grinding his teeth and cursing under his breath. He counted to three because there wasn't time to count to ten and reminded himself they *were* armor and didn't have the same limitations as *crunchies*. "Talon, you're approaching a defilade that hasn't been scouted out."

"Then we will recon by fire."

"Negative. Avoid. Go around."

"Fal'tir and the Talons will not delay. Talon, out."

"Gold to Talon, I say again, go around."

No response.

"Gold to Talon!"

Fallon counted the seconds, quickly learning the Dotari hadn't completely disregarded his warning. One of the war machines blasted the shadowed defilade with suppressive gauss fire while the others launched rockets into the camp. The sight of armor striding forward unleashing hell took his breath away.

As he checked to be sure none of the action was near his captured Marines or the rescue operation, a pair of Sanheel officers trotted near Baer's team.

"Baer you're about to get caught. Don't move. Ilyin, get ready."

"Way ahead of you, sir. But I only have one of them lined up. They've stopped at the corner of Lieutenant Baer's position."

On the far side of the artillery park, two of the Dotari Armor switched from rockets to gauss rounds into the defilade.

"We have problem," a Dotari voice announced.

Fallon hand-signaled Gold Squad onto a firing line, finishing with a fist displayed. "Hold."

"Green light?" Ilyin asked.

"Hold."

Kesaht tanks raced forward, dragging camouflage netting as their engines roared and turret gunners opened fire. Rakka warriors clung to rings on the outside of the bulky vehicles as dirt spilled off tank hulls and treads.

"Talon 4, contact. Tanks," a Dotari voice announced. "No problem."

"Yes problem," another Dotari said.

"Problem?"

"Not enough targets for Talons to destroy."

One Dotari Armor completed his missile salvo then joined

the rest of the lance facing the new threat.

Fallon swung his mag-viewer toward the parked Kesaht trucks where Baer and three other Marines remained hidden, ready to fight or move at the first opportunity, as Rakka and Sanheel gathered closer and closer to their position. A single line of trucks separated at least two platoons of Rakka from the four men.

Sanheel officers formed the Rakka ranks to respond to the Dotari attack. The front of the rushed, drunken column began to move.

As Fallon watched, one officer cantered around the line of trucks until something caught the alien centaur's attention.

"Ilyin, drop that prancing pony," Fallon said, quickly estimating odds of a stand-up fight if this went poorly.

The Sanheel stopped, twisting its long torso to look between trucks, then backed up as he raised a hand to summon his warriors.

Ilyin fired once and the Sanheel dropped sideways, hitting the ground hard enough to throw up dirt.

Fallon held his breath.

More Sanheel and Rakka continued toward the Dotari assault, screaming and chanting and beating their chests.

"Thanks," Baer said. "That was close."

Fallon pounded his fist as he saw what Baer and his rescue team couldn't. One Rakka—one idiotic, barbaric, drunk Rakka—stood near the fallen Sanheel officer, screaming and waving his hands, sounding the alert. More rushed to him. A Sanheel officer galloped to his fallen comrade and shouted orders.

"Ilyin, you are weapons free," Fallon ordered. "Start putting them down. Baer, get Antony and any other survivors out of there."

He tracked Baer's progress, watching as they engaged Rakka at close range, never slowing or diverting from their course. Enemies fell around them, dropped by sniper rounds.

Horns, drums, and klaxons sounded the alert, turning the Kesaht base into a kicked-over anthill.

Dotari Armor fell back in pairs, moving at angles from the tanks to force them to turn and lose momentum. Rakka troops jumped from the tanks and swarmed after them.

"Baer, what's your status?"

"On scene. One survivor. Repeat, one survivor."

Fallon's guts went hollow. "Get him and get out."

He watched his lieutenant punch one of the trucks and wave a fist just as a Rakka came around the truck. Baer lunged forward, jamming the barrel of his rifle into the Rakka's mouth and pulling the trigger. He shoved the body as it fell and went looking for more until one of his Marines pulled him back.

Baer went to a dead Marine and cut him down from the transport.

From his position, Fallon couldn't see who it was but spots of rage danced in his vision. The void continued to fill him as he counted the dead Marines.

"Just grab their dog tags! Don't cut them down. Damn it, Baer! I need you to get the hell out of there!"

"Moving," Baer growled over the comlink. His team

sprinted from the area, burdened by Antony's limp body.

"Tridents. Target priority: artillery emplacements, ammunition dump, then clear a path for Baer. Don't be stingy," Fallon said.

Two trident teams knelt on the ridge and shoulder-fired rockets aimed at the camp. They fired in sequence, one trident team reloading as the other attacked. The first rocket jumped into the air, fell slightly, then raced away as booster rockets flared to life. Fallon's sniper and other Strike Marines fired at a Sanheel-led mass of Rakka already charging toward the Marines' position.

Fallon checked the damage done to the Kesaht guns then swiped his mag-viewer toward the ammunition jump a second after it exploded. A fireball reached for the sky and secondary explosions bounced through the camp like angry demons on a suicide mission.

The tridents fired again, and again, then stopped.

"That's it, Colonel. We're dry."

"Grenade the tridents and get ready to move. We can't afford their weight," Fallon said.

"We can carry them back."

"Negative. This is going to be a sprint. I have more tridents than trident operators in Syracuse City. Form up and move out."

"We can't get back the way we came," Baer announced. "Send new rally-point coordinates."

Fallon consulted his computer maps, then looked up to scan the route he wanted to take. "Sending now. ETA five minutes."

"Received and understood. We'll be there in four."

Distant explosions marked the progress of the Dotari Armor. They had drawn the tanks up a steep slope, then jumped down on them, peeling away turrets and ripping crews from inside. More than one squadron of Kesaht tanks retreated while others began the laborious process of flanking in the difficult terrain.

Fal'tir and his lance again moved up the slope, dead bodies and wreckage strewn across the terrain below them.

Fallon checked on their progress whenever he wasn't attending to his own team. Not a young man, he had to push his armor to keep up with the younger Marines.

Fal'tir's Talons engaged two distinct masses of Kesaht with gauss fire and rockets while infantry swarmed up the slope and tanks fired from new positions.

"Gold to Talon, we are away. Get the hell out of there."

"No, Gold. You are not away. They must come to us and die so that you may return to the city and live."

"Talon, I have operational command. Fall back. Fight another day."

"Alas, Gold. I am touched by your concern for our welfare, but it is all bovine leavings. We must do this."

"Crimson to Gold, we're at the rally point," Baer advised.

Fallon pushed ahead of his security team to reach Baer. "Let me see him."

Baer said nothing. His eyes bore into Fallon's soul as medical team unfolded a stretcher and strapped Antony to it. Fallon stepped back to let them work, then reached for the dog tags Baer held. Baer pulled them a fraction of an inch closer to his body.

Baer realized what he had done and started to hand over the dog tags from the rest of Antony's team.

"Hold onto them, Lieutenant." Exhaustion moved through Fallon's bones, but he resisted the pull of fatigue and despair.

"We should have saved more of them. Now Antony's on death's door to die and I saw Marines die with my own eye," Baer said.

The words cut into Fallon's soul. "Wrong. We'd have lost them both if I unleashed our sniper and trident teams. I'd have lost you and your team with them. Unacceptable."

"You heartless bastard."

"This is war. War is suffering and heartache. Accept it and move on...we can grieve when the battle's over," Fallon said.

He barely heard his own words over the ringing in his ears. Images of Antony and his team running laps around the base filled his head, and then memories of his nephew, Lieutenant Raymond Fallon, crowded into the scene. He wondered if his nephew died because of another officer's call.

Baer saluted and turned to the stretcher team. "Let's go! Time's a'wastin'!"

Chapter 16

Two Rakka dragged a body by the heels. Grunting with effort and snorting at each other, they brought it into a Kesaht sick bay with dozens of raised slabs throughout the room. Rakka lay on each one, burnt, bleeding, some dead with loose limbs draped over the sides.

An Ixio in a deep-red body glove waved a hand over an injured foot soldier. A holo detailed the Rakka's wounds and the lithe alien pursed its thin lips.

"Treatment time to stabilize you is too long," the Ixio said. "Your service to the great cause is noted."

Putting a hand to the Rakka's forehead, he pinned it down and a spike thrust out of the slab and pierced the base of the Rakka's skull, killing it instantly. Orderlies in bloodstained smocks dragged their dead fellow away and brought another Rakka with burns across much of its left side to the slab.

"Hold." The Ixio turned to the pair bringing in the new body. They were on the verge of a fight, both hunched over and posturing, tusks bared, arms held to their sides.

"You two…" The Ixio sauntered over and the Rakka lowered their heads out of respect. "Where did you find that…thing?"

The Ixio stopped a few feet away from a massive body covered in burnt-out armor as one of the Rakka clawed at his mouth.

"Fly masters found," it said. "Bring you. Eat, yes?"

"No, I'm not going to eat this, you imbecile." The Ixio nudged the body with a foot and an armor plate on one arm fell off, revealing mottled flesh. "What is it? Too large to be the cursed human or a Dotari slave."

"Smell wrong," the other Rakka said. "Burn. Burn?"

"Put it on the slab." The Ixio gestured and a holo appeared in his hand of another of its kind. "Hecklana, come see what I've found."

"I'm in triage, Felgan. We cannot waste Lord Bale's servants," the other Ixio said.

"Lord Bale will be much more interested in this." Felgan turned his palm toward the body.

"I'll be right there. Don't start without me."

Felgan sniffed the air—a sweetness, almost like glycol—as the Rakka dragged Opal's body to the slab. He almost appreciated the scent. Anything was better than Rakka blood and voided bowels.

****

Hoffman leaned against a bulkhead and felt his heart racing as Max and Gor'al knelt next to the hole they'd cut out of a wall.

"That's the power line," Max said.

"No, the power lines have red and white stripes that—" Sparks hit Gor'al in the visor and he snapped his hands away from the wall. "Correction. That *is* a power line."

"This is not the time for discovery learning," King said. "Can you two access the ship's network or not?"

Gor'al connected a wire from his gauntlet to a data port and strings of text raced over the screen on his forearm.

"Cowabunga," Gor'al said.

Garrison raised a hand, then put it back on his rifle.

"I'm letting that one go. Been a long day."

"Most of the ship is still off-line," Gor'al said. "Upper decks are all exposed to vacuum and there are low-oxygen warnings." Small yellow points filled the wire diagram, matching the damage Hoffman saw during their approach.

"There access to the bridge or not?" Hoffman asked as a wire diagram of the Kesaht dreadnought appeared on his visor.

"Systems are largely intact around the command structure," Gor'al said, "but the fusion cores are in reboot. Should be another hour before they're online."

"Then the ship's weapons will be back online. That's how long the *Breitenfeld* has left," Hoffman said.

"They know we're here," King said. "We're in for a fight if

195

we try and get through the decks just beneath the command center."

"Get to the hull and EVA?" Hoffman asked.

"Fighters." King frowned. "We'd get caught in the open."

"You've conducted operations on large ships before," Gor'al said. "There must be a solution."

"*Kid'ran's Gift* and that Xaros drone were a shoestring tackle," Max said. "I feel like we've used up all our luck as it is."

"Garrison," Hoffman said, pointing to the explosives case behind the breacher, "how much damage can you cause with that?"

"Got nine kilograms of denethrite," Garrison said. "Depends where it explodes. Get me in someplace with atmo and we can factor in blast waves, fires, other collateral damage. We set it off here, we're just rearranging the rubble."

"We're not that far from the bridge," Hoffman said. "Gor'al, give me some options."

"Any sewer pipes?" Booker asked. "That was fun on the big Dotari ship. Don't think I ever got the smell out of my armor."

"There is a network of access tunnels running beneath every third deck," Gor'al said. "I suspect they send Rakka crew to wherever they're needed, but they're all sealed right now. We cut or blast our way through, we will garner attention. These menials don't seem to be that motivated to work…Now this is interesting."

"Spit it out," Duke said.

Gor'al tapped his screen and a compartment flashed on the diagram—one not far from where they were.

"This is a bit confusing, but it might be what we need.

Hmm…" Gor'al clicked his beak absentmindedly. "One moment, there are a lot of details in this Ixio schematic. Their language is both difficult and easy to read. By that I mean it is very exact and descriptive. I see many words that are new to me."

Hoffman's patience frayed as alien script appeared in the wire diagram. "Gor'al? Talk to me."

"It is labeled 'armory,' which is where munitions would be kept, yes? Would there not also be explosives—grenades, perhaps?"

"That'll work," Garrison said.

"Why is there an armory on the Rakka levels?" Booker asked. "The Kesaht officers don't seem to have a whole lot of trust when it comes to those brutes."

"Aliens…" Duke shrugged and gave Gor'al a sideways glance.

"Look here, boss," Max said, pinging a column running below the command center. "This lift is huge, probably either for heavy equipment or the Sanheel. There's a passageway from the armory. If we load that with explosives and send it up to the bridge level…"

"Or close enough to the bridge," Garrison said. "There's a generous margin of error when it comes to denethrite."

Hoffman slapped the breacher on the back. "You have that dangerous look in your eyes that always gets you in trouble."

Garrison braced himself for a rebuke but smiled cautiously.

"But let's plan for the worst-case scenario." Hoffman laid

197

out his plan and watched his team fill in the details.

****

The only lights in the Rakka tunnel were infrequent power indicators on some of the larger wiring conduits. It was like touring a ship museum that hadn't been cleaned—ever. Rust marked sections of grated flooring. Darkness swathed the Strike Marines. Night-vision filters gave everything a washed-out appearance.

"I'll take point," Duke said. "These tunnels are one long, low curve. I can't do overwatch in here. Might as well get some." He tapped the large knife secured on his armor between his hip and armpit.

"How long has it been since you were up front?" King asked, ducking under a pipe as he walked.

"How long has it been since we had a full team with a proper point element?" Duke asked, checking the bayonet attachment on his gauss carbine and moving forward.

"Max, go with him," Hoffman said.

"Yes, sir."

Hoffman, Booker, and Gor'al made up the center element and King brought up the rear.

The lieutenant felt a thump through his boots and a wave of air filled the tunnel. Sounds carried toward them—footfalls and grunts.

"Company," Duke said. "Menials, I think."

"Man, you have good hearing for an old guy," Max said.

"I'm forty-one, snowflake."

"Like I said, ancient. I think you're right though. Sounds like a work crew—lots of lifting and grunting by the sound of it," Max said. "They don't rate flashlights, apparently."

Hoffman and the others moved closer to the corner when the point element stopped. Ahead of them were a dozen unarmored Rakka loading crates onto a cart that had fallen over.

"Permission to take them out?" Duke asked.

Hoffman hesitated only for a second. If these workers raised the alarm, the mission would be in jeopardy. "Hold and see if they move on. If they don't, take them as silently as possible."

"We can do it with knives, but it will take all of us hitting at once," Duke said.

"Understood." Hoffman signaled the others to get ready.

"They're just doing their job," Max said in a flat voice.

"Right now, their job is to die," Duke said. "We're way behind enemy lines, in case you haven't noticed."

"I get it," Max said. "Just stating a fact."

"Now," Hoffman said, rushing forward with his team to fall on the unsuspecting Rakka menials. He covered the mouth of his victim and stabbed him just under the base of his skull, yanking him backward off his feet at the same time. The effect was to bury the blade to the hilt between the Rakka's neck vertebrae. He gave the blade a short, hard shake to make sure none of the neural impulses made it from brain to body.

The rest of his team lowered bodies to the ground, but Gor'al wore a grim expression. He'd slashed his victim's throat, creating the only mess during the attack. There had been blood from those killed by the Strike Marines, but much less.

"You must teach me how to do it your way," Gor'al said.

The team moved into the next part of the tunnel. The Rakka working this area were smaller than the warriors and the tunnels seemed to reflect that fact.

"They might send someone to investigate when all these work crews fail to show up," Booker said.

"The clock is ticking," Hoffman said. "Move out."

"This next section is really cramped. We need to climb through this hole and hope for the best," Duke said, in a voice just above a whisper.

Hoffman nodded. They were so close together now that radio comms were redundant.

"Let me switch with Max," King said.

"Max, take rearguard," Hoffman said.

"Yes, sir."

"I don't think Opal would have fit," Hoffman said and no one commented.

The team emerged into the next maintenance tunnel like wraiths twisting through a swamp. The area was illuminated by red light—barely enough for them to see the low, curving passage. A caravan of the worker dregs moved toward them, hunched over carts and grunting what could have been a near-wordless work song.

"There is just enough illumination to jack with my optics," Duke grumbled.

"Deal with it," King said.

When the first Rakka looked up and saw Duke and King, he stopped, causing others to ram their carts into him. One by one, they began to scream and scramble backward.

Duke fired, cursing as they ducked behind metal containers and fled through the doorway.

King had better luck, wounding two of the dregs. "Too cramped in here for a decent gun battle. It's like fighting in an elevator."

"This isn't going well," Garrison said. "I mean, our luck had to run out sooner or later."

"Thanks, meathead. Thanks a lot," Max said.

"Rakka warriors," Duke warned as a swarm of armored enemies rushed through the portal-like door, shoving aside the spilled crates. He swung his patrol carbine over his shoulder where it locked magnetically next to his sniper rifle. Without hesitation, he snapped his Ka-Bar from his gauntlet housing and lunged.

King shouldered a Rakka leader backward, pulled his entrenching tool from his kit, and split the leader's helmet.

Duke's blade caught his opponent in the throat right below the helmet edge.

Booker charged forward, scrambling over a crate and into the fray. She rammed the butt of her gauss rifle against the face shield of another Rakka warrior who was bending down to avoid bumping his head. Like the other Strike Marines, the pseudo-muscle layer gave her extra strength even if she lacked the weight of Garrison or King

Hunched down, Hoffman, Max, and Gor'al charged forward, bayonets snapping out from under their gauss rifle barrels.

Garrison laid out the biggest of the Rakka with his breaching tool, smashing the heel of it into his opponent's helmet, and though one Rakka managed to fire a shot, the rest seemed eager for hand-to-hand combat.

With a kick to his chest, Hoffman flew onto his back as Max was dragged down by a thick-shouldered Rakka who tried to strangle him with both hands.

"OK, now this is dumb," Max snarled, drawing his sidearm and firing three rounds into his attacker's armpit. Blood and flesh splattered the area behind his attacker before the brute fell on Max, who pushed and twisted to free himself quickly.

Duke flashed from one Rakka to another, blood streaking the air behind his knife. After dispatching his third victim, he popped open his helmet and spat chewing-tobacco juice into the corner. "All things being equal, I'd rather be sniping."

"You did all right," King said.

"They know we're down here. Time's a wastin'. Sound off," Hoffman said. "Who's injured?" When everyone was accounted for, he breathed a sigh of relief, though they'd taken a handful of minor damage. Booker glued Max's eyebrow back together; he'd been struck so hard he'd felt the blow inside his helmet. Everything else was twisted joints and strained muscles, nothing a medic could do much about in the field.

"Check your gear. We're not done," King said.

Their Strike Marine armor had taken far more damage

since boarding the super-dreadnought, so they fixed what they could and hurried under the armory.

"This is the place." Gor'al said. "I am certain."

Hoffman referred to his own maps and agreed.

Garrison laughed giddily as he looked up at the ceiling. "Bring on the unlimited supply of Kesaht ordnance." Taking a cutting torch from his breaching kit, he carved a hole big enough for Opal to crawl through, had he still been with them. Looking at his fellow Strike Marines, he said, "Habit. I forget he's not here anymore. I really miss that guy."

King and Duke lowered the cutout piece to the floor. Garrison boosted Booker up.

"It's dark. No alarms. No guards. We came up in what looks like a shower room, or maybe a morgue," she said. "Lots of metal tables and drains."

"Weird," Garrison said. "Any ordnance?"

"Not in this room. Push me up a few more inches," Booker said. Seconds later, she disappeared through the hole. "I'm dropping a line."

One by one the team made their way into the armory.

Hoffman scanned the new environment. "This isn't an armory. Something adjacent to it, I hope."

"Weird place for an infirmary," Max said, scanning the darkness through his rifle sights.

"It's not an infirmary," said Booker. "It's a morgue, like I said. There are metal tables and drains, but no life-support machines or medicine cabinets."

Hoffman pointed to the massive double doors at one end of the room. "Listen first, then run an IR optic line through the door gap. We'll hack the code or breach it manually if everything looks good on the other side. Max and Gor'al, you first. If you can't get it open, Garrison will have to muscle it with his pry tool."

Max and Gor'al moved to the double doors and studied the control panel.

"Not locked. I don't think anyone left in this room is supposed to be able to break out, being dead and all," Max said.

"I don't like this," King said.

"Do the Kesaht normally put their hospitals next to explosives?" Hoffman leaned close to Gor'al. "Are you sure about this?"

Gor'al shook his head, an action that would have rustled his quills if he hadn't been wearing a helmet. "The schematic said 'armory.' Kesaht are not concerned with the lives of their people, especially not the Rakka. They would not care if an accident with explosives killed wounded warriors in an adjacent facility."

"Open the doors, then stand back. Watch and wait. If they come at us in here, we need to kill a lot of them before they realize we're essentially cornered," Hoffman said.

"We can conduct a fighting retreat through the tunnels," King said, clearly unhappy with the idea.

"Let's hope we don't have to," Hoffman said.

The doors opened. Nothing happened. Hoffman hand-signaled the team forward in stealth mode. They moved slowly, careful not to make a noise or get caught by a light that would cast a shadow the wrong direction. King reached the barrel of his gauss rifle around the corner, using the aiming reticule to see what his eyes couldn't.

"Not… good," he said. "L-T, you better have a look."

"Send your rifle view to the team," Hoffman said. A few moments later he was watching a macabre scene in his HUD.

The room was huge, full of Rakka Armor being operated on. Several corpses were piled on metal tables that had been pushed into the corner. Too big for the tables, the armor squatted on the floor in what looked like stand-by mode. The alien-skull helmets were dark. Unlike the death machines Hoffman and the others faced on the *Breitenfeld*, these lacked lit eye sockets and electricity crackling between the exaggerated skull fangs. Oil dripped from gears as the weight of the armor squashed the hydraulics in ankles, knees, and hips.

Guns, flamethrower tubes, and melee weapons were attached to back plates. Hoffman couldn't tell if the ammunition belts were full or not.

Ixio technicians climbed up a ladder to the skull of one unit, removed a tube from the armor with a Rakka brain suspended within, and tossed it into a bin next to the Kesaht war machine.

"Gor'al, you got the word wrong," Hoffman whispered.

"Oops," Gor'al said. "The Ixio morphology is even more convoluted than my native language. Maybe their word for 'armory' means a place where armor is made? Yes, I think…"

Everyone in the team carefully and quietly turned their heads to look at him.

"'Oops' is not helping us," Booker said.

Gor'al made a dry hissing sound—similar to the way Dotari laughed, but different. "Is that not the appropriate response after making an honest mistake?"

"We'll talk later," Hoffman said.

"It *is* an armory, for Kesaht *Armor*," Max said, disgust and dread in his voice.

"We're screwed," Garrison said. "That's what I get for dreaming big. All the explosives you want. Blow up everything you see. More is better. Make the world burn!"

King slashed a knife hand through the air for silence.

Hoffman made the only viable choice he saw. "Advance. Don't be seen. There's no going back. We'll need to improvise."

His team stalked into the huge room, looking for other doors or passages that might lead them away from the Kesaht armor. The harsh lights above the operating tables at the far end of the cavernous, barrack-like area cast beams of light and shadow like a forest of diagonal trees. All the while, they watched Rakka brains being tossed aside before new ones were removed from coolers and installed into the armor units. Some of the metal tables were like three-tiered bunk beds where unconscious Rakka lay waiting to be vivisected. There were tall medical cabinets on wheels and a disorganized array of surgical support machines—IV bag holders, ventilators, and battery stacks.

"It's like a World War I sick bay from hell," Booker said.

"Or Satan's slaughterhouse," Duke added. "By the Saint, that stinks. My breather isn't filtering it out."

"Hold," Hoffman said as he picked up a new angle. "I'm seeing a whole lot of Kesaht Armor ready to switch on."

"We need to get out of here," King said.

"Thank you, Gunney Obvious," Booker said.

"We have a large, open area to cross. The tables and tool racks won't hide us from here to the opposite door," Hoffman said. "King, you'll take Garrison and Gor'al across first. Max and Booker next. Duke and I will bring up the rear. If we don't make it, find a way to disable this ship. This mission can't fail. Valdar and the fleet are depending on us."

No one argued.

King, Garrison, and Gor'al waited for the scientists to begin a new procedure.

"Go," King said as he rushed silently forward.

They were at the door when a Rakka guard turned and saw them.

"Contact!" King shouted a split second before he opened fire on the Kesaht security team. Hoffman and the others selected targets and fired on the move.

Duke fired a beat slower than the rest of the Strike Marines, but his rounds struck their enemies with unerring precision. Gauss rounds from the rest of the team cut down the scientists and their assistants before they could switch on the armor.

Ricochets caromed all through the cavernous medical barracks. Ventilators and vats of blood exploded messily. Two of the battery stacks used to jump-start the Kesaht Armor exploded, showering sparks and blinding Hoffman and the others. Helmet visors adjusted back and forth between bright light and the gloomy murk.

One Kesaht Armor unit squatted near the operating table but away from the "storage" area. It twitched, rising unsteadily to its feet as light appeared in its mechanical eyes. Hoffman now understood it was nothing more than a machine with a Rakka brain plugged in. His earlier confusion about where the pilot's womb was located was now resolved.

"Damn, we stepped in it this time!" Booker said.

"Yes! We have now taken the tiger by the horns!" Gor'al said.

"I love your enthusiasm but can you help us kill it?" King asked as he moved to cover, shooting with steady accuracy and a controlled rate of fire.

The rest of the Marines performed similarly, as they'd been trained, while Gor'al planted his feet and dumped a magazine into the body of the Kesaht Armor.

"Move! Move! Move!" King shouted at the Dotari Marine. "You have to shoot *and* move!"

Chapter 17

Felgan lifted a laser cutter from a tray and ran it along the seam underneath Opal's helmet. He pulled it away and peered down at the doughboy with his wide, black eyes.

From a slab across the room, a Rakka groaned in pain. The Ixio flicked overlong fingers toward the noise.

"End that one," he said to an orderly.

"Fighter. Minor hurt," said the Rakka, scraping a foot against the deck.

"Spike!" Felgan snapped and the orderly scampered away. There was a snap a moment later and the groaning ceased.

"What is this?" He poked Opal's face. "Skin doesn't match human norms. Subcutaneous fluid contains no DNA..."

"Did you start?" Hecklana asked as she walked up to the opposite side of the slab.

"Prep work. You did let me stand in on the Dotari examination." Felgan picked up a circular saw.

"This is uglier than most humans." Hecklana grabbed

209

Opal's chin and turned it from side to side. "What's that smell? So sweet."

"I believe it's blood. Or some ersatz liquid." Felgan spun up the saw.

"New species belong to Lord Bale," Hecklana said. "Vivisection is forbidden."

"*Prisoners* are Lord Bale's domain," Felgan said. "This one is dead. Recovered from the void by a rescue team searching for pilots. We must record this discovery for Lord Bale. He may want more subjects for additional…tests."

"Lord Bale is always interested in new meat." Hecklana put a clear face shield across her mouth.

The blade spun, blurring the air. Felgan lowered it toward the Terran creature's cranium.

The Ixio leaned close as the blade worked slowly into Opal's temple and dots of clear liquid spattered their faces.

Opal's eyes flashed open. His arms came up and snatched Felgan by the throat, swiping aside the saw. The tool went flying and bounced against the deck, the blade still spinning. The doughboy swung his feet over one side of the slab and got to his feet, lifting Felgan up like he weighed nothing at all. The Ixio kicked uselessly, his mouth open in a silent scream.

"Kill!" Opal snapped Felgan's neck with a twist of his wrist, screaming with such rage that his dry voice box seemed to tear apart from the sound. He slammed Felgan onto the slab, snapping bones and crushing the back of the alien's skull.

"Guards! Guards! Save me!" Hecklana shouted as she

picked up a laser scalpel and pointed it at Opal.

The doughboy snarled, grabbed the other side of the slab, and swung his feet over. He jumped toward the Ixio, landing right in front of her and clapping his meaty hands against the sides of her skull. The Ixio's head popped like a grape and she stood for a moment, the laser scalpel still en garde.

Opal's gaze snapped to a gaggle of Rakka orderlies. The aliens tried to flee through a doorway at once, confounding their escape in a mass of bodies.

The doughboy roared and charged the Rakka, beating fists against his chest.

Chapter 18

The Kesaht Armor came hard and fast, slamming operating tables and the few surviving Ixio scientists out of the way like rag dolls. One of the thinly built aliens flailed through the air and into a storage cabinet, falling in a tangle of arms and legs after the impact, blood spraying from its crushed face and broken hands.

"High-powered shots only. Make 'em count," Hoffman shouted as he moved behind a stack of industrial-strength surgical tools. "We saw them taking brains out of the chest cavity. That area will be heavily armored. The head may still be vulnerable as a sensor bundle or command relay," Hoffman said.

Rapid-fire slugs burst from the enemy's arm cannon, punching holes through equipment, walls, and Rakka warriors struggling up from their beds, their feeder tubes breaking away from the half-conscious aliens. They staggered forward, blind with rage and confusion. Other Rakka warriors rushed into the room from the main hallway, firing weapons ahead of them to clear a path.

Half-complete, the first of the metal behemoths still

towered above Hoffman and his team, though most of its gears were exposed and a piece of metal seemed to be missing between the shoulder plate and upper torso. Hoffman moved forward, looking for a way to exploit the weakness.

Max and Booker whirled to cut down the Rakka security team, exchanging rounds at near-point-blank range. Bullets caromed off both Strike Marines, causing injuries Hoffman couldn't see from his position.

"I'd like to use a grenade," Garrison shouted. He fired several times and moved. "Oh, that's right. We don't have anything explosive left. I feel so obsolete." He grabbed the mangled corpse of an Ixio scientist and held it up briefly as a shield. Ricochets and flying debris peppered the body, causing it to do a macabre dance. He dropped it and dove toward a recessed doorway for a sliver of cover. Pressing his body as flat as possible, he reloaded while cracking jokes in a high, whining voice.

Booker and Max sprinted from one medical cabinet to another, enemy rounds bursting through their meager cover as they leaned on each other for support.

Duke, King, Hoffman, and Garrison—still squawking complaints—opened fire at the same time, using their teammates' desperate flight as a distraction, their high-powered gauss rounds striking the neck and head of the Kesaht Armor. The skull-shaped head came off, bouncing across the deck like a metal football. The enemy unit continued to advance, its slug cannon sweeping side to side, destroying anything it pointed at while a nozzle opened on the other arm and sent a gout of flame against the ceiling.

"Spread out," Hoffman shouted. "It might be blind."

His team tried to comply, but the fire pinned them down. There were only so many places to go.

Hoffman dashed forward, unable to see the gap in the partially finished armor he had noticed a moment ago. Certain it was there, and desperate to exploit it, he zigzagged nearer as the metal giant stomped forward, shooting at random.

The rapid-fire slug thrower was so loud it overwhelmed the noise dampening within his helmet.

"I don't think this thing was meant to fight inside a ship," Garrison said, his loud voice barely heard over the noise.

"We let it rampage long enough, it'll do our job for us," Booker yelled. "Of course, we'll be dead. I've got a fractured arm, I think. Max got shot *again*. Evaluating."

Not liking the miserable sound of Booker's voice, Hoffman crossed the final distance in a rush, jamming the barrel of his rifle into the gap in the armor. One pull of the trigger sent a burst of rounds into the vulnerable braincase.

The Kesaht Armor reared backward, dragging Hoffman and his trapped rifle with him. He tried to let go but it was too late. His feet swung up into the air as the cannon arm continued to fire, doing more damage to the Rakka than the Strike Marines.

Bullets and explosions filled the room that had seemed too big less than a minute ago.

Something thick and wet splashed out of the braincase and Hoffman's rifle slipped free. He flew over a collection of overturned tables and landed hard on one hand and both knees.

His armor quivered as it absorbed the impact. He rolled away and moved to a new position, looking for another way out. All he found was a closed door that was shaking as though another Kesaht Armor unit was trying to break it down.

"L-T, behind you." King warned.

Hoffman turned in time to see another half-finished armor bearing down on him. It raised a foot and Hoffman spun away from the wall, just before it slammed its hoof-shaped boot down where he had been standing, the vibrations from the impact shaking him. He stumbled. The armor punched with its flamethrower fist, hitting the door that the unfriendly menace was trying to break down from the other side.

"We've got to get Max out of here!" Booker yelled.

Hoffman couldn't see her and wasn't sure how many times she had yelled before he heard the words. The Kesaht Armor had fixated on him. It alternated trying to shoot, stomp, or cook him. His team fired on the thing but couldn't put it down. There were holes and smoking wires in a dozen places, but the monster was relentless.

"Garrison, cover me. I have to do something," Booker ordered.

Hoffman caught a glimpse of Garrison and Gor'al shielding Booker with their bodies as she knelt over Max and pulled the tourniquet strap built into the leg of his Strike Marine armor. Hoffman couldn't figure out why none of his team was helping him with the Kesaht Armor…until he saw Duke and King fighting a new wave of Rakka soldiers gathered near the main

215

entrance.

Reflexively, his hand went to where he kept anti-tank grenades, but found nothing.

The Kesaht Armor swung a huge fist, winging Hoffman on the shoulder. The force was like getting bumped by a passing truck. He went down, spinning from the glancing blow.

The door behind him smashed open.

"Kill enemy!" roared a familiar voice.

Hoffman rolled sideways, avoiding a hoofed metal foot, and risked a glance to the door.

"Opal?" He rolled to the other side and dodged another crushing blow.

"Kill enemy!"

Opal, larger than life and mad as hell, launched himself at the Kesaht Armor. The doughboy had a length of metal in one hand that looked like it had been ripped from the ceiling. Opal rammed one pointed end into the Kesaht armor's torso, into the unarmored machine works.

The metal monstrosity staggered a step.

"No hurt sir!" Opal roared as he grabbed the armor by the elbow and pulled it off-balance. It fell to one side. Opal wrenched his improvised weapon out and stabbed it into the brain cavity in the upper shoulders of the headless armor, driving the jagged metal into the cavity again, pink liquid splashing against his chest.

The Kesaht Armor twitched as it died.

"More…" Opal turned toward the remaining Rakka at the door.

"Opal 6-1-9, stay with sir!" Hoffman ordered.

King and the others shot down the Rakka, who'd seemed to have lost the will to fight after Opal's arrival.

"You're alive?" Hoffman touched Opal's bare arm. His fingers came away slick with deep-blue blood. "And you've been busy."

"Sir ordered Opal to abandon ship." Opal tossed the metal bit aside. "Then explosion. Unit off-line due to oxygen loss. Found enemies."

The team gathered, exhaustion and injuries forgotten. Opal opened his arms and pulled King, Duke, and Hoffman into an embrace, lifting all three onto their toes.

"What did they do to him?" Garrison asked.

"Don't let him hug me," Max said, favoring one leg. "I don't do reunions well."

"Right, Max. No need to get all emotional," Garrison said, leaning back from one of Opal's reaching arms. "Hey, big guy. Hands off the goods. Getting crushed isn't really my thing."

"No hug?"

"No hug!"

Hoffman and the others laughed as the doughboy chased Garrison around the room. It was surreal, like being ripped from a space battle and plunged into a scene from basic training when they were all young and eager.

Hoffman felt lightheaded, not from being squeezed by the doughboy, but from the contrast between imminent destruction and this brief, intense happiness. He looked over his old companion, and a sense of dread filled his chest.

"Opal's armor is incomplete. We can't take him into the void," Hoffman said. Another monkey wrench in the works of his mission.

"And get some rockets from these Kesaht losers," Garrison said, already looting the Kesaht Armor and the security team of Rakka Marines.

Alarms, finally noticeable without the sounds of battle filling the room, blared from every room and hallway. Duke faced the nearest speaker, aimed, and put a gauss round through it.

"Sorry. It was messing up my Chi."

"I still want to know what they did to Opal," Garrison said. "That's not his blood, right?"

"Gor'al," Hoffman said, pointing a knife hand at the Dotari's midsection, "hack in and find us escape pods. That's how we'll get off this ship once we blow the command center. Garrison, you have enough denethrite?"

"Little goes a long way." He held up the case. "I'll use it all, if you don't mind. I'm getting sick of carrying the damn thing."

Hoffman picked up one of the Rakka's crudely made rifles and tossed it to Opal. The doughboy looked down at it and one corner of his mouth twitched.

"Better than your bare hands, Opie," the lieutenant said. "The enemy's confused, and nearly deaf and blind. This isn't time for a fair fight. Strike Marines, with me."

****

The Strike Marines hustled down a wide, smoky hallway to a tall set of doors where three different kinds of alien text shone from the frame: Sanskrit-like dashes, flowing text written in circles, and images so crude they struck Hoffman as little better than petroglyphs.

"This is the place," Gor'al said as he put his back to the bulkhead adjacent to the door.

"You sure?" Booker asked. "You tell us the sign says 'elevator' and we open up a Sanheel sauna, I'm going to feed you to Opal."

Opal held the Rakka weapon in one hand, which was almost comically small in his hands. The doughboy's chest heaved as smoke curled around his head.

"Take a knee." King tapped Opal on the shoulder and the battle construct complied, lowering his head to clearer air.

"Bad enough he's missing most of his armor," Max said. "None of us are meat shields."

"Get the door open." Hoffman waved Garrison forward and the breacher took his pry bar off the small of his back and jammed one end into the door seam. As he did, King noticed a bag made of rough cloth dangling from his equipment belt.

"Garrison, what the hell is that?" asked the sergeant.

"I found chow on a Rakka. He didn't look hungry." Garrison twisted the pry bar and got the door to pop open an inch. Smoke flowed into the room beyond.

"Are you sure it's food?" Booker asked. "It could be a

Kesaht colostomy bag for all you know."

"Ha ha, very funny. I'm still going to eat it," Garrison said. "Got it popped. Ready in three…"

Hoffman and Max wrapped their fingers around the open edges and hauled the sliding doors open on Garrison's count.

Inside was a large elevator column in the center of a circular room, ringed by heavy, vault-like doors.

"*There* is the elevator." Gor'al raised a finger. "Please don't feed me to the battle construct."

"Eat?" Opal was the first into the elevator room. He swept the muzzle of his weapon across two workstations along the near side wall and sidestepped around the elevator shaft.

"Room clear," he said.

"Secure the door." Hoffman went around the other side of the shaft and gave the vaults a quick once-over. "Garrison, set up the bomb. Gor'al, get the lift down here then find us a life pod."

The Dotari went to a workstation and hit a key. Screens lit up. "Should we get our horse-cart…cart-horse order correct? If there's no life pod then we won't—"

"We will," Hoffman snapped. "Strike Marines do not surrender. We win or we die trying."

"Then let us hope the Kesaht have some sense of self-preservation." The Dotari attached his gauntlet to a data port.

Garrison set down the explosives case next to the elevator doors and opened it. He took a detonator off his belt and tapped it against his helmet.

"I can go with a time fuse," he said, looking up to where

the shaft went into the ceiling, "or a command signal detonation. I don't know how long the trip will take to the bridge or if I can get a signal through. Decisions, decisions."

A white circle above the elevator door turned on and off.

"Gor'al, I'm not ready." Garrison plugged the detonator into the denethrite, a black material run through with golden strands.

"I have yet to access the elevator controls," the Dotari said.

There was a ping, and the doors opened. A squad of Sanheel shock troops charged out, knocking Garrison one way, the explosives another.

Opal fired his Rakka rifle, but the bullet sprang off a Sanheel's armor. He bared his teeth and swung it like a club toward a centaur's head. The Sanheel blocked the strike with a forearm and the rifle snapped in half. The Sanheel jumped, landing its front legs to one side, and kicked Opal in the chest with its rear hooves. The doughboy let out an *oomph* and went flying.

King and Max opened fire, their rounds snapping off the aliens' shields.

Hoffman shot from the hip, taking a Sanheel in the flank that blew out a hunk of flesh the size of his fist. The alien bucked, dropping his rifle and sending it clattering behind him. The lieutenant jumped onto the Sanheel's back and tried to get an arm around its neck. Spittle-covered tusks snapped at him as Hoffman held on for dear life.

Hoffman snapped his Ka-Bar blade from his gauntlet and

punched it into the alien's back. It cried in pain and swung an elbow around that whacked Hoffman across the jaw. Even with his helmet on, the blow sent stars across his vision. Hoffman wrenched his blade arm down and ripped the knife through Sanheel flesh and armor, severing the spinal column. The alien went down, landing on one side and pinning Hoffman's leg to the deck. Gauss fire and alien shouting filled the room as Hoffman tried to pull free.

He heard the smack of metal on metal behind him, and one of the other Sanheel was there, brandishing its long rifle with a serrated bayonet fixed. Gauss shells sprang off its shield as it raised its weapon up to stab Hoffman.

The air split with a sonic boom, sending a slap of overpressure that beat Hoffman's head against the deck.

The Sanheel about to murder him was missing from the waist up; its arms still clutching the weapon lay on the deck. A fine mist of alien blood settled around them.

King grabbed the lieutenant by the carry handle and dragged him out from under the Sanheel corpse.

"So loud!" Opal shouted. The doughboy sat against one of the vault doors, his hands cupped over his bare ears while Booker checked him over.

Duke hefted his smoking sniper rifle. "Who said I wasn't going to need this on a ship?" the sniper said.

The third Sanheel lay dead, riddled with gauss bullets, the overloaded shield snapping like a live wire.

"No no no!" Garrison dove to the elevator and slid inside

as it started to close. Max stomped a foot on the breacher's ankle, stopping him halfway in. The doors shut against Garrison's waist and the groan of gears sounded through the shaft.

"Help!" Garrison sat up and tried to pull the doors open, with no success.

Gor'al ran over and pushed a blue button on the shaft. The doors opened.

"Oh," Garrison said, half in and half out of the elevator. "I knew that. Bomb? Where's the bomb?"

"Here." Booker put a foot to the case and pushed it across the deck to Garrison.

"Same questions remain," Garrison said as he removed a time fuse from his belt. "Countdown? Command detonation?"

Something beat high against the chamber doors and more blows came below that. Hoffman was sure a force of Rakka led by a Sanheel was on the other side.

"Given the time between our arrival in this room and the security response," Gor'al said, hurrying back to the workstation, "I factor in the velocity and—"

"Grenades!" Max shouted. "Who's got a frag left?"

"Here," Booker said, tossing one to him.

"Booby trap." Max pointed at a Sanheel body.

"And a time fuse." Garrison shrugged. "And a wireless detonator. Let's make all the above work, yeah? I need one of those big uglies."

"Do it." Hoffman wiped aerosolized blood off his visor as a whistling sound caught his attention. Duke's rail rifle bullet had

223

passed clean through one of the vault doors, and air was being sucked through. He went to the hole and rapped the back of his hand against the metal.

He looked to Opal. The doughboy was breathing hard and he wasn't sure if it was from the hit he took or the air vacating the room.

Garrison moved the denethrite case into the elevator, then he, Max and Duke dragged the Sanheel Hoffman had killed into the elevator.

"Gor'al," Hoffman said, going to the Dotari, "what's behind those doors?"

"The system is acting up." Gor'al let off a series of agitated clicks. "I think the bridge is trying to cut the power to the elevator. We wish to rob a Kesaht bank?"

"Hurry!" Hoffman called out to the Marines in the elevator as they dragged the Sanheel corpse onto the denethrite case. Garrison flipped his frag grenade over and pressed a thumb against a button. There were four clicks, then he pulled the pin and wedged it between the corpse and the case.

"I set the grenade for instant detonation." Garrison skipped over the Sanheel and the other Marines got out. "Sure hope it's a smooth trip up—don't want that going off. Also got a five-minute timer that's running."

He looked at Gor'al and then back to the elevator.

"Now, you dip thief," Duke said. "The timer's running now!"

"Ah yes." Gor'al touched his gauntlet screen and the doors

shut. The elevator ascended with a hum of machinery.

Hoffman pointed to the dog—the wheel knob—on a vault door over Opal. It was too high for a Rakka to reach, but just right for a Sanheel.

"Open that."

Opal got up and gripped the wheel with both hands. Muscles rippled down his back and arms, then the vault popped open. A pod. One with four Sanheel-sized crash seats.

"This is most amusing," Gor'al said, his gaze locked on his gauntlet screen.

"Gor'al," Hoffman said as he waved his team into the escape pod.

"This was barely an inconvenience," the Dotari said. "We're in the escape-pod room. I must reroute a number of power commands to trip the fail safes and—"

Hoffman grabbed him by the arm and dragged him to the pod.

"Or we just open the door and leave. Also that." The Dotari shrugged his arm loose and ran to the pod.

Hoffman was the last one in. As the Marines looked over the alien setup, Booker pulled a facemask with a tube out from under a seat and gave it to Opal.

The forward end of the pod was concentric rings of windows looking down a dark tube.

"You'd think there'd be some big red button," Duke said, lifting up a seat cushion. "Escape pods shouldn't be complicated."

"Here." Max flipped a panel down revealing a spike-covered handle inside. "Weird, but here goes nothing." He pulled the handle and it came down with a pop. A hatch shut over the doorway and a magnetic hum filled the air.

"Hold on to something," Hoffman said.

The pod kicked forward, slamming the Marines back in a jumble of limbs.

Chapter 19

Valdar's lift came to a sudden stop, the doors half-open to the bridge, the deck level with the admiral's chest. Valdar gripped the ledge and jumped up and onto the bridge, rolling to a stop.

"Elevators are a bit hit-and-miss," Egan said as Valdar walked up to the holo tank, where a depiction of the ship wavered with static.

"You don't say." Valdar tapped a screen and it flickered on and off. "Stack three is a complete loss. Power junctions down the prow are shorted out. Repairs will take another forty-seven minutes."

"Some good news," Egan said, handing a slate to Valdar that displayed a picture of the dreadnought, the pyramid bridge structure blasted away, atmosphere venting out from a massive hull breach.

"I'm not chalking this up to good luck," Valdar said. "Hoffman?"

"Looks like something he'd do," Egan said with smile.

"Strike Marines aren't ones to sit on their hands, waiting for instructions."

"I never doubted him. What's the status on the hull repairs?"

"EVA teams are—" Egan stopped as a white plane of light emerged in the void.

"Wormhole!" Utrecht shouted.

Valdar hit two knuckles against the holo table. If the Kesaht had just sent reinforcements, then it was all over for him and his ship. He hoped that wasn't the case. He wanted a nobler end for the *Breitenfeld*, something better than a helpless target hanging in the void.

Ships emerged from the wormhole and a cheer went through the bridge. The hulls of Terran Union ships were easy to make out against the quantum bridge as it faded away.

"Egan, get them on the horn," Valdar said. "We need those ships fighting over Syracuse. The more force we bring to bear, the less our casualties."

"Aye aye," the XO said.

The new arrivals' engines came alive and they burned a course straight toward the *Breitenfeld*. Shuttles emerged from the strike carrier at the center of the formation and sped ahead.

"No answer to our hails." Egan shook his head. "The IR transmitter must have been damaged in that near miss. Switching to auxiliaries."

Valdar pulled camera feed from the forward point-defense turrets. Images of a half-dozen Mule transports, afterburners alight, came up in the holo tank. The ships were packed close together, heading straight toward a single turret. As he watched, the image jumped around.

"Are they jinking?" Valdar asked. "It's like they're on an assault vector."

"Still nothing from the auxiliary channels…" Egan did a double take at the Mules in the tank. "What the hell is that?" He reached into the holo and rewound the footage. A fighter was just beneath one of the Mules, the hull black and red with stubby, forward-swept wings.

"That's not one of ours," Egan said.

Valdar stopped the feed again and zoomed in on a unit symbol painted on the aileron of a Mule: a red Crusader cross on a white shield.

"Ibarrans," Valdar said, dread hitting him like a punch to the gut. "Prepare to repel boarders. Now. Ship-wide alert!"

Lights switched to a pulsating crimson and Valdar drew a gauss pistol from his thigh holster.

"Armsmen are stuck in the lifts," Egan said.

"Protect the Keystone," Valdar said. "It's the only thing that matters."

An icon flashed on Valdar's visor. A hail from the Ibarran ships.

"Now they want to talk," Egan said.

"XO…prep the self-destruct sequence," Valdar said.

"Wait. What?"

"We can't let them get the Keystone. Get to it. I'll stall for time." Valdar looked Egan straight in the eye, his determination evident.

"Aye aye," Egan said, putting a hand to the side of his helmet.

Valdar opened the channel and a young, attractive woman with alabaster skin and deep-red lips appeared on his visor screen. Hair the color of the abyss was done up neatly behind her head.

"Admiral Valdar of the *Breitenfeld*," she said with a faint accent. "I am Makarov. Ibarran Nation vessel *Warsaw*. Prepare to receive my legionnaires and turn over control of your ship."

"Makarov...I heard about you."

"You served with my mother. As a professional courtesy...I'll give you one chance to stand down. You are dead in space. You have no means to resist," she said, throwing at him the words from the Terran Union's code of conduct against surrender. "My men do not wish to harm you or your crew, but any resistance will be met with deadly force. Surrender. Now."

"You're after the wrong ship, ghost." Valdar cut the transmission just as an Ibarran Mule swept past the bridge.

"Battery stacks one and two are spooling up," Egan said, his eyes wide and on the edge of fear. "Another two minutes before we can trip the breakers and send them into meltdown."

Valdar lifted a panel and put his hand to a yellow-and-black striped screen. A sensor read his biometrics through his glove and it slid aside revealing a red handle within.

"Get to yours, Egan," Valdar said. The XO went to the opposite side of the holo tank controls and repeated the process.

230

Small icons for two of the three battery stacks pulsed amber, a gauge filling slowly within each.

"Not how I thought this would go," Egan said. "But it's been an honor, sir."

"The honor's mine, Egan." Valdar gripped the handle...and stopped as the charge icons for both battery stacks froze.

Valdar opened a channel to the battery room. When no one answered, he triggered the screen override. Video from the stacks' control station came up, and tall, black-armored soldiers stepped over the bullet-ridden bodies of Valdar's sailors.

"God damn—"

A bulkhead exploded inward, sending a door-sized section barreling across the bridge and into the lift doors. Valdar brought his gauss pistol toward the breach just as a dazzler grenade exploded. His visor went dark automatically, blocking most of the blast, but enough of the harsh light left a pulsing afterimage across his eyes.

Valdar fired blindly and backpedaled. He bumped into the tank controls and made out a hulking shape. A hand gripped his shoulder and he fired again, just before a blow struck him across the face and sent him flying through the holo. He hit the deck hard and shook the flash from his eyes.

Snaps of gauss fire played across the floor. He looked through the bottom of the holo tank and saw a half-dozen boarders working through the breach. Valdar looked to his hand and was surprised to still see his pistol. He fired into the mass of attackers. The gauss shells sprang off armor but more than one hit home and sent loose gouts of blood and air.

"Admiral!" Egan shouted.

Valdar reloaded his weapon and stood.

Egan, the former Strike Marine, had a gauss carbine, and he swung the stock against the helm of a dark-armored boarder, a red Crusader cross emblazoned on his visor. Egan's blow hit home and turned the Ibarran's head around so fast the rest of his body twisted. As he crumbled, another Ibarran fired over the body, the bullet striking Egan in the chest and sending the XO back a step.

Egan made an ugly noise, then charged forward. An Ibarran kicked him in the stomach so hard Egan doubled over. A blow to the back of the head sent him to the deck.

Valdar aimed his pistol forward and pulled the trigger, but a hand knocked the gun up, sending the bullet into the ceiling. Valdar stepped back and twisted the pistol toward an Ibarran with wide shoulders, his face hidden behind a bright-red cross. The Ibarran chopped a hand against Valdar's wrist and the pistol went flying as another hand shot out and grabbed Valdar by the neck.

The Ibarran lifted the admiral off the deck, then slammed him against the bulkhead, rattling Valdar's skull against his helmet. His world went fuzzy for a moment and then his entire body went down hard on the deck.

An Ibarran loomed over the admiral, then slapped a small circle against the side of his helm. Valdar's void suit locked up, freezing him in place. His ears rang with blood and he felt a warm trickle down the side of his face.

Makarov appeared on his visor.

"I'm disappointed in you, Valdar," she said. "But I'm not surprised. You were never one to back down from the impossible. But this time...this time you failed."

"What do you want from me?"

"You? We don't want you or your ship." A slight smile played across her face. "Lady Ibarra demands the Keystone you've got in your hold and your flight deck. Seeing as I don't have all the time in the world to unload it, I'll just take the *Breitenfeld* and the Keystone back back to Ibarran space as a package. She'll make a fine addition to the Nation's navy. Don't you think?"

"You don't deserve her! This ship won the Ember War and if you think—"

"Earth abandoned the mantle to defend all of humanity. The Lady took on that responsibility...it's only right she has your ship as well. God is with *us* now, Valdar," said Makarov, and she vanished.

Valdar struggled against his own void suit, powerless and defeated.

Chapter 20

Fallon and his Marines reached Devastator just as the sun came up. They moved through a forest, adjacent to a plain full of a Kesaht assault force massing on the rail gun. The perimeter was breached in several places, and crescent fighters strafed the emplacement, dodging sporadic return fire.

"Gold to Garrison, do you read me?" Fallon asked over Devastator's IR command channel.

"Garrison 1, go," Franks replied.

"Status?"

Franks answered but the radio static and noise from explosions made his words unintelligible.

"They've been under direct assault for hours, I think," Baer said.

"That's my assessment as well." Fallon took in the chaotic scene. "Gold 1 to all unit commanders, our priorities are as follows: keep the Devastator firing, repulse enemy forces, strengthen perimeter defenses."

"Unit commanders are acknowledging," Baer reported,

then tackled Fallon as two crescent fighters dropped low and opened fire.

Fallon saw stars when they hit the ground and then Baer popped to his feet and started dragging him. Fallon heaved himself into a nearly upright posture and started running as more crescent fighters strafed his position and semitranslucent blaster fire whizzed past Baer. Fallon felt enemy rounds cutting the air near his face as dirt exploded from the ground.

A Marine cried out. Fallon turned back to help the injured man but couldn't find him.

"Colonel!" Baer grabbed him, dragged him to a crater, and threw him in.

Fallon landed badly, ignored the pain, and righted himself as Baer took cover.

"Medic!" a voice cried out.

"Move! Move! Move!" another shouted.

"Why isn't that air-defense gun firing?" Fallon said, already running toward it as Baer and another Marine followed. Fallon prayed they wouldn't get blasted in the next strafing run.

He jumped up three steps, then scrambled behind the blast shield. Two dead Marines and a militiaman lay in a pool of blood, tangled in their body parts. He grabbed one, hefted him up, and dumped him outside the turret. "Baer! Help me get this thing up!"

The Strike Marine Lieutenant squeezed past him and chucked the other two bodies out, his face grim with anger and determination.

Fallon dropped into the gunner's seat, splashing blood in

all directions. Baer loaded a new magazine, then bent over the radar screen. "They're coming around for another pass."

"I see the sons a bitches," Fallon said, the air-defense gun drowning out his words. He pulled on the handles to elevate the barrels as he jammed his right foot down on a pedal and lifted his left foot slightly. The turret spun, tossing Baer sideways. The big Marine grabbed a handrail, then strapped himself in as Fallon continued firing.

Tracer rounds slashed into the sky. He aggressively adjusted his aim, blowing off the nose of the lead crescent fighter, sending it to the ground where it exploded. The pilot's wingman shot over Fallon's position, energy beams blasting the ground all around them.

"Two more at nine o'clock!" Baer shouted.

Fallon jammed his left foot down hard and hydraulics and gears spun the air-defense gun. He felt like he was on a rollercoaster or launch simulator. "I don't see it."

"It's moving fast."

Fallon searched through the targeting reticle, sweeping it across a sky increasingly filled with enemy fighters. When something flashed across his peripheral vision, he followed, aimed, and fired, the rounds pounding the side of a crescent fighter. A long second after multiple impacts, the ship exploded in the air.

A klaxon blared from the Devastator, audible through the din of battle and Fallon's ringing ears. He glanced toward the massive rail gun where it was thrusting up from its bunker complex.

Fallon fired at another group of fighters but missed.

A gust of wind cleared smoke from the scene and Fallon stared at the ladder into the turret, not remembering it or the blood all around the air-defense gun. The bodies were another story.

"I need the dog tags from those men."

"I'll write the letters," Baer said.

"The hell you will. My command. My responsibility." Fallon forced his gaze toward the Devastator as its alert system gave three final tones. "If that thing goes down, our mission was pointless."

A giant Kesaht ship came over the horizon, contrasting against the golden dawn.

"That's a big ship," Baer said.

"A big, dead ship if we're lucky. All we need is one good shot."

The Kesaht ship fired every forward gun it possessed, illuminating the sky with green energy and shredding the air with kinetic rounds. Fallon and Baer ducked behind the turret shield, flinching as the heat passed over them on the way to its target.

The Kesaht barrage blazed over Syracuse City toward the Devastator and kept going.

"Clean miss!" Baer shouted.

Fallon watched the Kesaht ordnance hit the mountains beyond the city, throwing up mushroom clouds at the same moment the Devastator fired back. Shockwaves radiated from the railgun and the ground jumped several inches. Fallon staggered and gripped the gun controls, feeling like his fillings had been knocked loose.

"Damn, that's what a rail gun at full power feels like!" Baer shouted, hands over the ear sections of his helmet.

Fallon held his breath as the nearly translucent beam cut the lower atmosphere, flashing across several kilometers in a second, slamming through the fuselage of the titanically huge Kesaht lander. The ship split and the rear half seemed to spin slowly on one engine that hadn't given up. Several parts fell to the earth like slow-moving rocks while the front half took a nosedive for the surface.

"Hell yeah!" Baer shouted. "There had to be an army of the Rakka bastards on that thing!"

An explosion filled the sky as the final engine went nuclear.

Fallon smiled to himself, awed by the power of a single gun. Laughing with a giddy mixture of exhaustion and hope, he pushed the barrel of the air-defense gun downward.

"Good work, Marines! Give'em hell," Fallon broadcast on all channels. "Damn fine work. This is what Syracuse stands for. Send those Kesaht jackwagons straight to hell."

Baer reloaded the magazine, then put one hand over his earpiece as he screened battlefield information for the colonel. "Kesaht fighters are breaking off. The Rakka didn't seem to get the memo. They're massing for an attack."

"I've got something for them," Fallon said as he waited for the ammunition to cycle up from the magazine beneath the turret. The moment it turned green, his eyes lit up, and he opened fire, blasting a row of charging Rakka into red mist.

The brutes charged his position in greater and greater numbers, insects drawn to a flame or fanatics seeking death. He slaughtered them.

Baer reloaded as fast as he could. "I think I'm getting the hang of this."

Teeth clenched, Fallon swept the barrels from left to right, striking Rakka warriors from less than three meters. Blood rained down on the turret, splashed across the next wave of death-hungry enemies, and turned the field around the air-defense gun to red mud.

"That's it. Magazine's dry," Baer said.

Fallon shoved himself away from the controls and climbed out, with Baer following. They ran toward the trenches.

"Get dirty, Marines!" Fallon shouted as he dropped behind a mixed group of Strike Marines and local militia. One of them was a teenage boy shaking so violently he could barely aim, but he did manage to fire into the fresh wave of Rakka.

"Baer, I want someone to put down that Sanheel officer two hundred meters out at two o'clock," Fallon said.

"Ilyin, you heard the colonel," Baer said.

"So pushy," the sniper said.

Fallon turned his attention closer to the trench before seeing if Ilyin hit his target. Rakka were rushing forward with bayonets, stepping on falling comrades and screaming in their harsh battle language

He moved beside the kid with the shaking rifle and spoke

239

as he aimed. "You got this, kid. Aim a bit low, take them in the hips or torso. Don't rush, just keep shooting. I'm right beside you doing the same thing."

"Yes, sir!" the kid said, his voice cracking.

Baer moved down the trench, intercepting a pair of Rakka jumping onto the sandbag rim of the defensive line. He shot one at close range, but the other Rakka was above him, getting ready to jump down. Baer slammed his gauntlet into his pelvis, yelling, "Get back down there!"

Fallon shouted, "Reloading!"

"Am I supposed to do that when I reload?" the kid asked.

"Just keep killing them!"

A squad of Strike Marines joined Fallon.

"Morning, Colonel," the squad leader said.

"Morning, Jake." Fallon plucked a grenade from the man's kit, armed it, and pitched it into the enemy ranks. "I'm all out."

"My grenades are your grenades, Colonel." He aimed his gauss rifle over the sandbags and opened fire.

"Reloading!" a Marine shouted.

"Covering!"

Baer rounded up ammunition from several militiamen and gave it to the Strike Marines.

"No offense," Baer said. "My guys are better shots. Fix bayonets. You're going to need them in about five seconds."

Fallon stepped back. "I'm out of ammo," he said, drawing the combat knife from the sleeve of his armor.

A cry went up farther down the line. "Rakka in trenches!

Enemy in the trenches!"

"Follow me!" Fallon shouted, then ran toward the breach. "If you're shooting, keep shooting. If you're not, fix bayonets and let's get to killing these assholes!"

Exhaustion seeped through the adrenaline right before the melee began. He stabbed with his combat knife, then slammed his elbow into his opponent. Baer shoved him forward, using their combined weight to unbalance the Rakka group leader.

Fallon stepped on him, turning his ankle painfully but not slowing down as Marines and militiamen lunged forward with bayonets. Fallon drew his pistol and fired at point-blank targets.

Something exploded.

Smoke filled the air.

Chunks of dirt rained down on them.

Fallon found himself alone with Rakka all around him. He fired his pistol dry, stabbed until he was sure the blade would snap, and hammered helmets with the barrel of his pistol until his arm felt like lead.

Baer appeared through the smoke, a Rakka held above his head.

"Don't drop that thing on me," Fallon grunted.

Baer pitched his flailing victim out of the trench as Strike Marines surrounded Fallon.

"It would be a lot easier for us if you were an REMF right now," Baer said.

"Well, that's just tough cookies, isn't it?"

****

Fallon took full magazines out of an ammo crate and snapped them onto his belt, forcing himself to reload despite the overwhelming need to sit down—maybe lay down, maybe just die right here. Silence held the battlefield. From what his fuzzy brain remembered of war, that was probably a good thing.

He slammed in the magazine, checked it, then holstered his pistol. Next came his rifle, which he slung over his back once it was combat ready. Looking around, he saw a defender struggling to get out of the trench. It took two pulls to get the man out.

Patting the man on the thick armor of his shoulder, he realized this was one of his Strike Marines, not a volunteer unused to battle fatigue. "Good work, Marine."

"Thanks, Colonel. Did we win?"

"We'll see. Find a medic. Get yourself checked out." Fallon walked along the trench, talking to those who could hear him, fist-bumping those who'd been deafened when the explosions became too much for the sound baffles in their gear.

"Gold for Crimson, what's your location?" Fallon asked.

"Crimson, I'm working my way to your position. With respect, sir, you're hard to keep up with for an old guy," Baer said.

"And you think talk like that will get you a promotion? We need to work on your attitude, Lieutenant."

Spotting a group of men, women, and teenagers looking for something to do, he waved them over. "Refill sandbags and stack them along the outer rim of the trench. Don't stop until an officer gives you another assignment. I'll send a team with water and rations."

"Okay. Who are you?"

"Get to work," Fallon said, moving on.

Baer joined him. "Orders, sir?"

"Get ready for the next fight. Because there's always one more fight."

Chapter 21

Hoffman and his Strike Marines marched onto a mesa as wind swept lines of sand across the smoothed-out tableau. The lieutenant looked back into a valley with a few scrub trees to where the escape pod had come to earth. They'd buried the parachute and covered the pod up with brush as best they could.

"This is awesome," Garrison said. "A dry heat. No snow. No ice. No freezing my huevos off when my armor loses power."

"You're such a baby." Booker rolled her eyes.

"Did *you* walk halfway across Koen in the dead of winter?" Garrison leveled a finger at her. "No. You were busy being a sniper and getting rides. Sitting in hot tents. Eating actual food. Wolves ever try and eat you? No. No they did not. Speaking of, anyone know if Syracuse has nasty things with pointy teeth?"

"Did I tell you all how nice the hospital on Koen was?" Max asked. "While I was getting my innards put back together. They had a decent movie stream."

"I forgot you shirked out of that whole mess," Duke said.

"Don't be bitter," Max said. "You like being planet-side.

Maybe you can snipe something to get in a better mood. Oh, look! There's a savage-looking squirrel. Save us from the small mammals, *White Fate*."

"Maybe we'll luck out and something will swallow Garrison whole," Booker said.

"Max? Comms status?" Hoffman asked.

"Not getting a damn thing." Max touched his earpiece as antennae worked up and down from his backpack. "Kesaht normally fritz the atmo of any planet they hit. Takes a few days to clear out."

"We're not going to sit here," Hoffman said. "There's still a fight on for this planet and we're still Marines. Even if we have…"

"Five rounds of gauss rifle ammo per weapon," King said. "Duke has two full magazines. Cross-leveled suit battery power to last forty-seven hours of continuous work."

"Which way?" Duke asked. "No GPS. None of us know the terrain to orient ourselves."

"The pod maneuvered of its own volition during our descent," Gor'al said. "Likely directing us toward Kesaht forces. It would make sense to drop escapees near 'friendly' forces."

"Make every shot count," King said.

"There," Hoffman said, pointing to the northern sky where distant flashes from explosions dotted the horizon. "The fight's that way."

"Walking…fun." Garrison looked up at the sky, which was tan with blown dust. Thunder sounded over the mountains.

245

****

Wiping sweat from his brow, Hoffman led his team down a sand-bottomed ravine and glanced back at Opal. The doughboy looked like a barbarian in his remaining armor. Streaks of alien blood remained even after getting caught in brief thunderstorms that had passed over them since they landed.

King increased his pace and caught up with the lieutenant.

"How's morale?" Hoffman asked.

"No one's complaining," King said.

"That bad."

"Team's been through extended ops before. Got to keep putting one foot in front of the other. No one's going to quit…you good, sir?"

"Why wouldn't I be? We disabled the Kesaht ship. This battle might still turn out for the good guys if the Dotari fleet performed as advertised." He looked to the darkening horizon. Signs of battle had ended hours ago, though it was still a question as to which fleet had met its end.

"And Opal?" King asked.

"He's been better," Hoffman said sadly. "Physical damage causes his system to degrade. We'll have him reboot when we get a chance."

"Contact," Duke said, the word going through the team's earpieces.

Hoffman and King took cover next to a boulder and the

lieutenant pulled an eyepiece up from his neck. A marked spot a few dozen yards ahead flashed on the small screen.

"Prone Rakka," Duke said. "Over by that pile of rocks. Body temp is low. Likely dead."

"Could still be more around here," Hoffman said. "I'm going to take a look."

He came around the boulder at a crouch and hurried to the body. The corpse was facedown in the sand, rifle in hand and water bottles hanging from pelts. Hoffman did a quick thermal scan of the plain that opened up beyond the ravine and the pile of rocks against the edge of the path from Hoffman to the Rakka.

"Looks clear," he said, and Max and Garrison came up to the other side of the ravine end and took overwatch.

Hoffman ran to the body and kicked it in the ribs. Rigor mortis had set in and the body barely moved from the blow. A massive exit wound exposed broken ribs.

"What killed you?" Hoffman knelt by the body and looked out across the plain. When he heard a rumble of falling rocks, Hoffman whirled around.

He stared down two gauss cannon barrels attached to a metal arm sticking out from the rock pile. A suit of armor stood up, dust and pebbles falling away as it reached its full height of fifteen feet. The armor kept its weapon trained on Hoffman.

"You are not Rakka," a Dotari voice said.

"Neither are we!" Garrison shouted and thumbed his rifle to high-power setting.

The armor snapped its gauss cannons back.

"Fal'tir," came from the armor.

"Hoffman. We've come across a few other enemy dead. Your doing?" Hoffman asked as he stood and flashed an OK sign to King.

"My lance saw a Kesaht escape pod break atmo. We decided to hunt Rakka stragglers while we investigated," Fal'tir said.

"That was us. The enemy loaned us a ride off their dreadnought," Hoffman said.

"You were *on* their ship…now you're here," the Dotari said.

"It's less fun than it sounds."

"Then there is no reason for any of us to remain in the field. I will recall my lance. Would you like a ride back to Devastator base?"

"Did I hear the words 'ride' and 'base'?" Garrison asked. "The worst ride is better than the best walk. I take back every bad thing I've ever said about Dotari."

"You what?" Gor'al asked. "Was 'tweety bird' not a term of endearment?"

Fal'tir's legs transformed into treads and the armor settled down into the sand, his helm now just a few feet higher than Hoffman's.

"Get on…crunchies."

Chapter 22

The hood came off Valdar's head and someone pushed him from behind. He stumbled into a jail cell of bare concrete walls and a single bunk bolted to the wall. He whirled around as bars slammed shut.

A pair of Ibarran guards armed with shock mauls regarded him for a moment, then left through a single door that shut with a whine of hydraulics as the vault-like enclosure locked. Beside him was another cell, but a privacy screen blocked him from seeing just beyond the other cell's bars.

Valdar looked up at the light recessed into the ceiling, then to the thin mattress on his bunk. Poking out from under the pillow was the corner of a small chap book, the cover reinforced with strips of tape. Writing from a thick marker had smudged and faded across the front. He opened it and found it was a Templar hymnal, property of one B. Bassani.

"What the hell is this?" Valdar tossed the book onto the mattress and looked around. No windows. No other way in or out but the vault door. He didn't see an air vent, but the air around him had chilled.

"My, my," a woman's voice came from behind him. "What a day."

Valdar turned. The privacy screen between the cells had fallen, and a woman in a robe sat on the other bunk. Her skin was silver, reflecting the light of the cells, and her hair, which was the same color, was frozen in a short cut that stopped just below her jawline. Her features were set like a doll's, but Valdar could see the soul behind her eyes.

His breath fogged with each exhalation and frostbite nipped at his ears. He knew her—had known her since she was a junior officer serving about the *Breitenfeld* under a fake name. Now she was something more than human, something far worse than he'd ever thought possible.

"Stacey Ibarra." Valdar crossed his arms over his chest.

"Been so long, Admiral." She stood, frost cracking from where her foot touched the floor. "Granted, our situations never did allow for us to catch up. Last I saw you was Ambassador Pa'lon's funeral, yes?"

"If you're in that cell," Valdar said, "then who's in charge of your Ibarra Nation?"

"Brass tacks," she said, dipping her face forward slightly, "still the man I knew. I wanted some quality time with you. One on one. I think you deserve that."

Stacey went to the cell door, wrapped a single hand around a bar and pulled it off the hinges with barely a trace of effort.

Setting the door to one side, she stepped out and took a few steps closer to Valdar. The chill worsened.

The admiral held his ground as he fought to keep his body from shivering.

"What have you done to my crew?" Valdar asked as frost grew amidst his beard.

Stacey squeezed the sleeve of her robe and the cold ebbed away.

"They're comfortable. The injured have been treated and they'll spend the rest of the war in a prison camp. No harm will come to them—which is a better deal than what the Terran Union's sworn to do if they capture any of my children," she said. "They call it the Omega Provision, but you and I both know it's murder. I wonder, Admiral, if you could have convinced President Garret to abandon that part of Earth's treaty with the rest of the galaxy."

"I don't know what you mean," Valdar said, fighting the urge to stick his aching hands into his pockets.

"Most everyone in my Nation was born against the provisions of the Hale Treaty. The Terran Union's holding to it. Every word." Stacey put her fingertips onto a bar and ice crystals formed beneath her touch. "Would you carry out that order, Admiral? When does duty overrule your morals? Historically, you haven't supported those in the Ibarra Nation."

Valdar's face flushed despite the cold. Years ago, during the first Toth incursion to Earth, he'd worked with a group trying to rid humanity of procedurally generated humans. Stacey's grandfather, Marc, had uncovered the plot and held that dishonor over Valdar's head for years.

"I know where my loyalties are, Stacey," he said. "I don't believe Garret would sanction the out-and-out killing of—"

"It's already happened!" Stacey snapped the bar in half. "My children dead at Terran Union hands simply for existing. Now I need to know if you'd carry out that order. Don't hesitate—you'd only insult me."

"I would not," Valdar said. "Killing in a battle is one thing. The Terran Union does not murder prisoners. Does not carry out mass slaughter. And don't you dare claim the moral high ground, Ibarra. I know what you did to the Toth. I was there!"

"That…" She looked away. "That was a necessary evil, Admiral. The Xaros Masters were gone, but their drones remained. We had a bargain to end the threat of the drones…and the Toth were sacrificed to balance the scales."

"It was genocide," Valdar said. "An entire alien race obliterated for—"

"Don't act like the Toth deserved respect or mercy," she snapped. "You know what they are. What they feed on. What they would have done to humanity if you and the 8th Fleet hadn't beaten them in the skies over Earth. There was no better solution. But you got your wish. A single Toth overlord survived. And now that one leads the Kesaht in a holy war against humanity."

"What?" Valdar sank to the bunk, the blanket stiff from the cold. "That can't be…"

"The overlord jumped out of the Toth home system

before the…purge. He went to the Kesaht system and recruited them to his cause, claiming humanity was a xenocidal species bent on destroying all life in the galaxy. Half-truths are always the worst lies, aren't they?"

"It's your fault the Kesaht are at war with us," Valdar said.

"The law of unintended consequences." She shrugged. "*I* didn't let the overlord go. I've wondered if our ally that day was playing a little game with us."

"You mean Malal," Valdar said, and a shiver went down his spine as he remembered the ancient, malevolent alien entity.

"The war against the Kesaht is coming to a head," Stacey said. "Earth is in danger, but I've found something that will turn the tide in our favor, something that will end the fighting with one swift stroke. Something beyond the reach of everyone in the galaxy…but me."

"The Keystone." Valdar looked up at her. "That's why you came for my ship. You needed the Keystone."

"Of course," she said, cocking her head slightly to one side. "You and the *Breitenfeld* were never the prize. I'm not so sentimental."

"Then why are you even here? You were never the type to gloat."

"You and your ship are legend," Stacey said. "The ship of miracles. *Gott mit uns.* My officers believe you can be…persuaded."

"Join you? Never."

"You put everything at risk when you first saved the Dotari years ago on Takeni," she said. "Then you jumped at the

253

chance to save them by rescuing the Golden Fleet in the deep void. This is for Earth. For all of humanity. Ibarran and Union."

She reached into her robe and pulled out a rank insignia shaped into a starburst with golden rays.

"Be with us as we win the war," she said. "Take the helm of the *Breitenfeld* again and be the hero we need. The hero you are."

Valdar looked at the rank and swallowed hard.

"You," he said slowly, "your grandfather, everyone that defected with you and everyone you've created for your 'nation'...are traitors. I will never help you. I will never fight beside you. And I will never command a ship in your name."

Stacey closed her hand into a fist, crushing the rank insignia to dust.

"I promised my officers I would try." She turned her palm over and let the pulverized rank slip to the floor like sand down an hour glass. "No more chances for you, Admiral. You'll spend the rest of the war in this cell. I may trade you for our prisoners held by Earth. Or I may use you as a tit for tat if the Union insists on murdering Ibarrans."

"If I'm a prisoner of war, then there's nothing left for me to say to you," Valdar said.

"I gave you a chance out of respect, because of our history together. You've chosen this cell...and that's all you'll get from me. We are done, Valdar." She gave his cell a quick glance. "Enjoy."

Stacey Ibarra went to the cell door and it opened so fast she didn't have to adjust her stride as she left. The door slammed shut.

Valdar touched the metal where Stacey had broken the bar, then shook the painful cold off his fingers. Looking to the hymn book and then to the other cell, he wondered who else had been here before him…and how they'd made it out.

"*Gott mit uns.*" Valdar looked to the ceiling and said a prayer for his ship and her crew.

Chapter 23

Fal'tir rolled up to Devastator's outer perimeter, and Hoffman and his team piled onto the skirt on top of Fal'tir's treads and of a second armor. The tall rail gun vanes stretched into the sky, a sentinel in the night. A thick column of smoke rose off to one side of the encampment around the massive weapon, blotting out stars.

"Look, little girl," Duke said, giving Ice Claw a pat, "it's your big brother."

Lieutenant Baer ran over, his rifle slung behind his back.

Hoffman bit his lip before he could chew the planetary defense force officer for not being battle ready. The time it would take to get his rifle in hand and ready to fire could be the difference between life and death. That he had his weapon stowed either meant the man was a fool…or the battle was over.

The exhausted, faraway look in Baer's eyes told Hoffman it was the latter.

"More Strike Marines?" Baer asked. "How the hell'd you get here?"

"We took the scenic route," Hoffman said as he jumped off Fal'tir. "Thanks for the lift."

"Be well, Hoffman." Fal'tir beat a fist to his breastplate in salute.

"You look like hammered shit," Baer said. "But the colonel won't care. He'll want to see you ASAP, get an update from the fleet. We got ammo, batteries and a hot chow line for the rest of your guys."

He did a double take at Opal. "Sweet Jesus, is that what I think it is?" Baer asked.

"He's had a bad day. He normally greets people with a hug and a smile." Hoffman looked over one shoulder and Gunney King was already leading the rest of the team into the perimeter.

"Where's this colonel?" Hoffman asked.

Baer led him into the camp. The defenders looked exhausted, but there was a jubilant air, one of victory.

Hoffman sniffed. "You said you had hot chow. That some local BBQ?" he asked.

"Rakka." Baer shrugged. "Got to get rid of the bodies before they're more of a health hazard dead than they were alive."

They went into a trench line and Baer jerked a thumb to a dugout. The colonel was staring at a map with his back to the open door, his hands planted on a table.

Hoffman stepped in, stomped one foot to the ground, saluted and said, "Lieutenant Hoffman, reporting as ordered."

The colonel stiffened, then turned slowly. The older man snapped a return salute and marched over to Hoffman, staring at the dirt-stained name stenciled to his armor.

"What are the odds…" the colonel said.

"Sir?"

"Colonel Heinrich Fallon."

"Fallon?" Hoffman's brows rose and memories of the lieutenant who'd died on the *Kid'ran's Gift* came back to him. "Fallon…"

"You knew my nephew," the colonel said. A statement. Not a question.

"Yes, sir, served with him under Captain Bradford, God rest their souls."

"So, you're Thomas Hoffman?" the colonel asked.

"Yes, sir."

"The doughboy babysitter."

Hoffman didn't respond.

The colonel went back to the map table and leaned against it. He folded his arms across his chest and stared down Hoffman.

"My nephew said you were a sloppy, reckless Marine who could barely hold his commission."

"We were not friends, sir," Hoffman said.

"His last mission was classified," Fallon said. "Total loss of the Marines assigned to the *Breitenfeld* except for your team. And you all vanished after the *Breitenfeld* returned from deep space."

"We were reassigned to black ops." Hoffman felt like he'd already said too much, but he'd watched the colonel's nephew die. "Been on commo blackout since—"

"How did he die?" Fallon snapped. "All his mother got

258

was an estimated date he was KIA and that enemy action was involved. Nothing else. My brother's widow has been broken since her child died, and the brass don't see it fit to share the details with us. Meanwhile, *you*—by all accounts a screwup—survive and go on to pull down assignments Strike Marines could only dream of."

Certain details of the mission to rescue the Dotari Golden Fleet were still highly classified, and Hoffman knew he could use that as a shield against the irate colonel. But Hoffman wasn't an intelligence officer. Lying was never acceptable in his book.

"I'll tell you, sir. Just don't let it get beyond Fallon's—"

The colonel held up a hand and nodded.

"He was on a separate assault point with the company commander to secure the bridge of a Dotari ship in deep space. My mission was to another location, but once we got aboard, we found that some of the Dotari had been transformed into banshees by a Xaros drone."

"What? That's impossible. The drones were destroyed at the end of the Ember War."

"The self-destruct signal that came from the Crucibles across the galaxy travels at the speed of light. The message hadn't reached that part of deep space yet. You understand why details were kept from the public?"

"If the Xaros still exist…then…my God." Fallon pinched the bridge of his nose.

"I led an assault on the bridge. There I encountered your nephew and other Marines coopted by the drone. There was nothing I could do for him," Hoffman said.

"But he died fighting?"

"Yes, sir."

"And you destroyed the drone?"

"Saw it disintegrate with my own two eyes."

Fallon nodded quickly then sat in a metal folding chair. He glanced over at a coffee pot, hot and full to the brim.

"Help yourself," Fallon said, rubbing a hand down his stubble. "You keep telling yourself you want to know. To get closure. But at the end of the day, it doesn't…the hole's still there."

Hoffman poured two cups of black and passed one over.

"He was a good Marine, sir, even if he did hate my guts."

"You seem all right," Fallon said. "How'd you get here? I thought the Crucible was still off-line."

"Came in on the *Breitenfeld*." Hoffman took a sip and was surprised by how something so bitter could taste so sweet after combat.

The colonel looked up at him, confusion writ across his face. "You weren't on the ship when the Ibarrans hit it?"

"The Ibarrans, sir?"

Fallon's face turned to stone.

****

Garrison lifted a tray of steaming food up to his face and breathed in deep through his nose.

"Mashed potatoes and mixed vegetables." He sat down next to the rest of his team, all chowing down. "Country-fried steak! The best reheated and rehydrated food the Terran Union can produce. All for us."

"You going to eat that?" Booker reached a fork toward Garrison's meat.

He slapped her hand. "I'll cut you."

The team ate in silence. Gor'al caught many a second glance as he picked at his vegetables.

Hoffman threw the flap to the mess tent open. Any trace of fatigue was gone as he walked down the rows of tables to his Marines, his eyes hard.

"Eat up," Garrison said, shoving half his steak into his mouth and chewing furiously.

"Oh, he looks mad." Duke pushed his empty tray away and put a bit of dip between his cheek and jowl. Gor'al sniffed at the air. "Try it and I'll do worse than cut you, Dotty."

Hoffman came to the end of the team's table and his Strike Marines got to their feet.

"Valdar's Hammers," he said. "We have a new mission."

THE END

Hoffman's Strike Marines return in *The Beast of Eridu,* out now!

FROM THE AUTHORS

Hello Dear and Gentle Reader,

Thank you for reading Valdar's Hammer. We hope you enjoyed Lieutenant Hoffman and his team's adventure, much more on the way!

Please leave a review on Amazon and let us know how we've done as storytellers, you're feedback is important to us.

Drop us a line at Richard@richardfoxauthor.com and scottmoonwritesanovel@gmail.com.

Also By Richard Fox:

The Ember War Saga:

1. The Ember War

2. The Ruins of Anthalas

3. Blood of Heroes

4. Earth Defiant

5. The Gardens of Nibiru

6. The Battle of the Void

7. The Siege of Earth

8. The Crucible

9. The Xaros Reckoning

Terran Armor Corps:

1. Iron Dragoons

2. The Ibarra Sanction

3. The True Measure

4. A House Divided

5. The Last Aeon

6. Ferrum Corde (Coming fall 2018!)

The Exiled Fleet Series:

1. Albion Lost

2. The Long March

3. Their Finest Hour (Coming 2018!)

About Scott Moon

Scott Moon has been writing fantasy and science fiction for over thirty-six years. When not reading, writing, or spending time with his awesome family, he enjoys playing the guitar, Brazilian Jiu Jitsu, and watching movies. Dog guy. Fan of the military. A career law enforcement officer, he served on the SWAT team, Gang Unit, Exploited Missing Child Unit, and helped catch a serial killer. He is also a co-host of the popular Keystroke Medium show (www.KeyStrokeMedium.com)

More Books and Stories by Scott Moon

The Chronicles of Kin Roland

Enemy of Man
Son of Orlan
Weapons of Earth

Read the entire Chronicles of Kin Roland trilogy on Kindle Unlimited!

SMC Marauders
Bayonet Dawn
Burning Sun

Son of a Dragonslayer
Dragon Badge
Dragon Attack
Dragon Land

The Fall of Promisdale
Death by Werewolf

Grendel Uprising

Proof of Death
Blood Royal
Grendel

Darklanding
Episode 1: Assignment Darklanding
Episode 2: Ike Shot the Sheriff
Episode 3: Outlaws
Episode 4: Runaway
(A new episode of Darklanding will be published every 18 days!)

Please visit http://www.ScottMoonWriter.com for more information.

Join the Scott Moon Group on Facebook to talk about books and stuff:
https://www.facebook.com/groups/ScottMoonGroup/

Printed in Great Britain
by Amazon